Story of Love

A Braden Novella

Love in Bloom Series

Melissa Foster

ISBN-10: 1-941480-72-1
ISBN-13: 978-1-941480-72-4

STORY OF LOVE

Cover Design: Elizabeth Mackey Designs & Natasha Brown

WORLD LITERARY PRESS
PRINTED IN THE UNITED STATES OF AMERICA

Dear Readers,

If this is your first Love in Bloom book, get ready to meet the loving and loyal Bradens of Weston, Colorado. *Story of Love* is a great way to get to know the family, and then you can go back and read each of their love stories.

See my website to start the Love in Bloom series FREE.

Sign up for my newsletter to receive a free Braden/Remington short story, and to be notified of new releases and events: www.MelissaFoster.com/News

Happy reading!
Melissa

Chapter One

RILEY BANKS RAN through the dark alley clutching a box of homemade brownies in one hand—*because every bride needs chocolate to calm her nerves*—and clinging to her fiancé with the other. If the last twenty-four hours were any indication of what her wedding day would be like, she'd need about ten more pounds of chocolate just to make it through the weekend. Warm air whisked over her skin as they fled the gorgeous Bahamas resort to avoid a mob of paparazzi that were eagerly awaiting the wedding of world-renowned fashion designer Josh Braden.

"This is so ridiculous, running away in the middle of the night like we're criminals. We're just two regular people who want to get married. It's not like we're celebrities." As Josh's business partner and codesigner, Riley was not far behind him in notoriety, but she didn't see herself that way. In her eyes, she was still a small-town girl from Weston, Colorado, who'd fallen in love with her high school crush years after graduation and happened to have a knack for designing clothes.

"No celebrity could hold a candle to you, babe." Josh tightened his grip on her hand, keeping her moving at a quick pace.

They rushed toward the road where Josh's brother Hugh

was waiting to drive them to a remote landing strip. There they'd connect with their brother-in-law Jack Remington, who would fly them to their *real* wedding destination—the Sterling House, a rustic inn where Josh's parents had been wed, in the Colorado mountains. The Sterling House no longer functioned as an inn, making it the ideal location to exchange their vows, for both sentimentality and privacy. Thankfully, Josh's extended family was happy to help them avoid the paparazzi mayhem. His relatives from Peaceful Harbor, Maryland, and Trusty, Colorado, had descended upon the resort for their fake wedding. Josh's cousin Jake was a stuntman and was used to the media swarming film sets and parties. He knew exactly how to create diversions *and* handle the media—giving Josh and Riley the chance to slip away unnoticed for the small, private ceremony they desperately desired.

Josh stopped suddenly and swept Riley into his arms. Love and adoration swam in his dark eyes, making Riley want to head back to the hotel and make love to him one more time before leaving the beautiful island.

"Are you having second thoughts about marrying a famous fashion designer? Because if you are, I'll go riches to rags and we can live on an island far away from paparazzi without a stitch of clothing or a dollar to our names."

Riley's heart swelled. She'd loved Josh for so long. She couldn't remember a time when she hadn't loved him, and she knew he would do anything for her—including giving up the incredible empire he'd created, which she'd never, *ever* want him to do. Although the *without a stitch of clothing* part sounded pretty darn good to her.

"No second thoughts about us, Josh. You know that." She glanced back at the sparkling lights of the resort against the clear night sky, then down at the cobblestones beneath their feet, and finally, she lifted her gaze to meet his, and her heart tumbled anew. She hated that the press had the ability to drive them away from such a romantic setting. The truth was, there were *many* times she resented the media attention that came along with Josh's fame. She wanted desperately for them to have a normal life together, one where they could walk in the park or go out to dinner without having to worry about photographers or reporters documenting their every move.

"I just can't imagine raising children under these conditions," she admitted for the tenth time in as many days.

Josh splayed his hand over her belly, and her body tingled with excitement—and worry. "I still can't believe we're pregnant."

When she'd stopped using birth control, she'd gone two months without having her period. Her doctor had assured her that her body was simply adjusting to going off the pill and from the stress of the elaborate scheme they'd concocted for their wedding.

"I'll never forget how devastated we were when the doctor said I would be unable to get pregnant." After three months without a period, her doctor had run tests, and he'd informed her that it appeared she had a rare condition called silent anovulation, where her body had regular periods but didn't release eggs. Apparently the pill had kept her cycle regular, and once she went off it, and her body was self-regulating, she didn't have periods at all.

"Can you believe it's been eight weeks?" They had still been mourning the children they'd never have when she'd started getting sick in the mornings and they'd run more tests. She placed her hand over his, remembering the elation that came with the news of her pregnancy.

"You're my medical miracle." He kissed her softly.

Her doctor had called her a medical anomaly. Her morning sickness, like everything else about this pregnancy, had been odd and had lasted only two weeks. Because of her doctor's concern over her unusual pregnancy, she and Josh had decided not to tell their families until they'd made it through the first trimester, at which time her doctor felt they would be past the most tenuous stage of pregnancy.

Josh bent down and kissed her not-yet-round belly, then rose and kissed her mouth softly. "I know you're worried. You know I'm all for moving back to Weston for part of the year if that's what you want. I'd do anything for you. For *both* of you."

It was true, he would. But as much as she wanted to raise their children in their hometown, near family and friends, neither of them knew what type of impact such a move would have on their business. And she couldn't get past the fact that asking Josh to move was unfair. The woman he'd fallen in love with had accepted *everything* about his life, including living in New York City and the media attention that came with it. She felt guilty for even thinking about moving away from the hub of the empire he'd built.

Despite the guilt, her heart raced just thinking about the idea of living in two places. She loved the idea of it, but she just couldn't figure out how they could possibly make it work. "I know you would, but dragging kids back and forth? Assuming we're lucky enough to have more than one. How hard will that be on *them*? And what about when they start school? We'd have to hire someone to handle the on-site management of the company while we're gone, and I don't want our kids raised by nannies because we're traveling all the time. I want them with us." Her mind felt like it might explode. There were too many things to consider and no easy answers. And to top it all off, she was on the cusp of launching a new clothing line next summer, which presented another host of issues to consider with a baby in the mix.

She splayed her hand protectively over her belly and took a deep breath. "I can't even think clearly enough to pull it all together. It seems like we're heading into a storm of unknown factors, and—"

Josh touched his lips to hers, silencing her fast-streaming words. Then he flashed that sexy, confident smile that made her insides flutter. "Babe, we will figure this out. We'll talk with Treat and Max, and Savannah and Jack, and the others. Look at Hugh and Brianna. They travel all the time with two children. And Dane and Lacy live on a boat. They're never in one place for more than a few weeks. If my siblings can maintain more than one household with children in tow, we can make it work, too." Of Josh's five siblings, only his brother Rex, and Rex's wife, Jade—Riley's best friend—had made Weston their only home.

"But their businesses are different and—"

He pressed his lips to hers again. "Shh, baby. Slow your brilliant mind for a second. Mia has been my assistant forever, and you know she can handle the office and coordinate schedules. It's not like we'll be in a third-world country with no Internet or phones. We can speak with her daily and fly back when necessary."

She clung to him, acutely aware of the seconds ticking by and Hugh and Jack waiting for them. Josh was her rock, and had been her calming influence during the craziest of times. He had the innate ability to see past chaos to the eye of the storm and diffuse it effortlessly. He was also the most accommodating man she'd ever met, and that knowledge came with responsibility. What if their business suffered because they weren't on site to oversee the production of the designs? What if schedules were problematic and caused issues with last-minute meetings like the ones they were always pulled in to? She didn't want to be the cause of making a mistake where their design firm was concerned.

"I'm still thinking about everything. Can you imagine how protective I'll be over our baby if we stay in the city? I'd probably get thrown in jail for clocking a photographer, or end up like Michael Jackson, covering our baby's face in veils so it's not put on the cover of every rag magazine. My claws still come out over the rest of the world wanting a piece of *you*." She wrung her hands together, unable to believe she'd just admitted something so juvenile.

He chuckled, and the enticing, low rumble gave her goose bumps. They'd been together for years, and she still found everything about him as exciting as she had on their very first date. He ran his hands over her hips, keeping her close—her favorite place—and brushed his lips over hers.

"They want a piece of *us*," he whispered. "You and I are one. And I know how much you hate the attention. I hate it, too, and I'd be the one in jail, because there's nothing I won't do to protect our family."

Ever since they'd gotten together, the media had begun snapping pictures of her when she was out doing the most mundane things—going for a walk or grocery shopping—and Josh had become more possessive than ever.

"But we have months to figure all of this out. And right now"—his gaze turned sinful—"you look so hot and sexy worrying about our baby. I want a piece of *us*, too."

He sealed his lips over hers, taking her in a heart-pounding kiss. She melted into the warmth and security of his arms, and her worries began to fade away. He clutched her ass, pressing her tighter against his growing arousal, and they both groaned.

"God I love you," he said hastily between kisses. His hands traveled up her back as he deepened the kiss.

"Christ, you two."

She startled at the sound of Hugh's deep voice, but when she tried to pull away, Josh intensified the kiss, leaving her no choice but to give in to his scintillating demands.

"For crying out loud," Hugh complained, though Riley could hear the smile in his voice. "You can make out in the car."

Ignoring Hugh's complaint, Josh's eyes turned serious. "Let me worry about the future. Think of nothing but our beautiful…" A silent "baby" passed between them. "Wedding. Okay?"

"*Christ*," Hugh grumbled. "Yeah, she gets it. We've got to get moving." He put a hand on Riley's back and guided her out of the alley. Like all the Braden men, Hugh and Josh shared their father's dark hair and eyes and his tall, broad stature. Only their sister, Savannah, had gotten their mother's auburn hair and eyes that hovered between green and hazel.

"We need to hurry," Hugh urged. "Jake just called and said the photogs are scrambling because someone thought they spotted Riley heading into town. They might have gotten wind of your escape."

"Hands off my woman, little brother." Josh's tone was only half teasing as his hand replaced Hugh's on Riley's back. With his mouth beside Riley's ear, he said, "You're my pretty *mama*."

A little thrill ran through her at his secret endearment *and* his staking claim—even if he had no reason to do so around his very married, very faithful, father-of-two brother.

"They didn't get wind of us," she assured them as they rushed across an empty street, following Hugh toward an off-road vehicle. "There was a last-minute addition to the plan. Your cousin Emily and a few of the girls headed toward town after we left to distract any lingering photographers. We thought it would help. The girls probably forgot to clue Jake in."

Hugh unlocked the doors as he called Jake and filled him in. Josh climbed into the backseat beside Riley, and she snuggled against him.

"Are you ready to ride off into the wild blue yonder and stop living in sin?" She read the answer in his eyes before he said a word. After watching Josh's five siblings and her best friend, Jade, marry and begin their families, she could hardly believe it was finally their turn.

Lacing her fingers with his, she imagined the adorable dark-haired baby they'd have. A baby with Josh's handsome features and easygoing nature and her spark of country-girl rebellion. A hint of fear and *what if* tiptoed in. She hated that the fear of losing the baby was never far behind her happier thoughts of what it would be like to love and cherish their child. As she'd been doing since the day she found out she was pregnant, she relied on that leap of faith her mother had told her about when she'd fallen in love with Josh, remembering their conversation as if it were yesterday. *"All you can be certain of is the here and now…It's all a leap of faith."*

"I've been ready for years. How about you?" He leaned closer and whispered, "Ready to make little, sweet hazel-eyed Rileys who wrap me around their tiny fingers and baby Joshes who are more interested in helping us design their birthday outfits than in riding ponies?"

Josh's voice pulled her from one memory to the next. She remembered the evening he'd proposed to her in Christos. At the time she'd thought that would be the biggest, most important event of her life other than the day they actually got married. But now she knew how very wrong she'd been. Each and every day they were together she experienced moments that felt bigger than any that came before them: When he climbed into the shower with her, hot and sweaty from his morning runs, hungry for her and *only* her. The way he gazed at her across the room when they were at fashion events, the electricity between them stronger than ever. And the loving words he whispered on a daily basis—none of which were sweet nothings. They were *sweet everythings.*

"Yes," she said, a little breathless. "I'll follow you anywhere your heart desires."

He nuzzled against her neck as Hugh sped down the dark, deserted roads, his breath warming her skin. "Being with you, babe, that's what I desire. Always and forever."

JOSH AWOKE AS the plane keeled toward the small private landing strip, giving him a bird's-eye view of the Sterling House. Sunlight spread like a misty blanket over the mountain peaks and the roof of the ancient inn, reflecting off the heart-shaped lake and reminding Josh of the reason they'd chosen to marry there. He'd lost his mother, Adriana, to cancer when he was just four years old, leaving his father, Hal, to raise him and his siblings on their family ranch. During the weeks when he and Riley were selecting a wedding venue, his mother had come to him in a dream. She had looked beautiful and young in her white wedding gown, standing before that very same lake, her long auburn hair blowing in a gentle breeze as she beckoned him with one hand. Josh was sure he had conjured up his mother's image out of sheer longing, wishing she could experience this momentous time with them. Truth be told, he had always been a little envious of his older siblings for having memories of their mother to draw upon, while he'd been too young to retain any. When he'd mentioned the dream to Riley, she'd been sure it was a sign. Until that dream, Josh wasn't so sure he believed in signs or spiritual connections, but his future wife did, and that was reason enough for him to agree—and to hope she was right.

"It's pretty cool that you chose to get married here," Hugh said softly, eyeing Riley, fast asleep beside Josh. "Do you think Mom and Dad knew when they married that they'd have six kids?" Hugh had been three when they'd lost their mother, and like Josh, he hadn't retained his memories of her. Treat was nine when their mother first became ill, and eleven when she died. He'd shared his treasured memories with each of them. Though Josh carried a little emptiness inside him for not having his own memories to draw from, he would forever be thankful to his family for helping him keep their mother's spirit alive.

Josh faced Hugh, thinking not of the question he'd asked, but of the unspoken one that lingered heavily between them. *Do you think they had any idea Mom would die so young?* Hugh watched him with a thoughtful expression. There had been a time when Hugh was all about chasing the next thrill, and there had been no place in his life for deep thoughts or serious relationships. He'd changed so much since falling in love with his wife, Brianna. Josh had a hard time imagining the responsible father of two Hugh had become as the wild child he'd grown up with.

With everything he'd been told about their spiritually connected mother, Josh was pretty sure she'd have had an inkling about how many children she'd have and about her life being cut short. But he kept the latter to himself.

"Dad said they always wanted a big family. Mom's been on my mind a lot lately," Josh admitted. "I wish she were here, you know? Not just for me, but for Dad." Their father swore he still communicated with their mother through Hope, the horse he'd given her when she first got sick. Some people thought that was a little crazy, but ever since Josh's dream, which had seemed so real, he was no longer sure.

Hugh nodded. "She is, bro. She's everywhere. When Christian was born I felt like she was right there with us." His little boy, Christian, was a handful, like Hugh had been as a curious, active child. Hugh had adopted Brianna's daughter, Layla, and the sweet, beautiful girl called him Daddy or Prince Hugh (an inside joke from her princess stage), and adored him just as much as Hugh adored her.

Josh couldn't wait to have his own family, and raise them with the love of his life. He had the same concerns Riley did about raising a family in the city, living in two locations, and traipsing all over the world for their fashion shows with, hopefully, more than one child in tow. He'd grown up with the benefit of strong family roots, in a small town where neighbors were always willing to lend a hand and everyone knew each other's business. That grapevine could be annoying, but there was comfort in it, too. His father still lived in their childhood home, and even after all these years, it brought a sense of security when he visited. And there was no denying that when he was back in Weston he felt closest to the mother he never had a chance to know. If only the answer to where they should live was as easy as falling in love with Riley had been. Once he fell, there was no turning back.

The plane descended and Riley stirred beside him. Thinking of his mother, a heavy feeling came over him. He loved Riley so immensely the thought of spending a single day without her pained him. How had his father survived without the woman he loved for all these years? How had he held his shit together when he had six grieving children relying on him? If anything ever happened to Riley, Josh wasn't sure he was strong enough to carry on with the fortitude his father had.

He kissed her temple, sending a silent prayer up to the heavens that he would never have to test his strength. "Hey, babe. We're landing."

She smiled up at him as the plane touched down. Glancing toward the front of the plane, where Jack was focused on piloting them to safety, she said, "We owe so much to your family for doing all of this. Poor Jack has been flying all night, and Hugh"—she looked at his brother—"thank you for helping us get to the plane and giving up a night with your family."

"It was my pleasure. It's about time my brother made an honest woman out of you," Hugh teased.

Riley snuggled closer to Josh. "He's been trying for years, but there was always something going on at work standing in our way. But we're here now, and we're more than ready. Did you guys get any sleep?"

"A little, but we're fine," Josh answered.

"We'll crash early tonight," Hugh added. "It's not like we'll have anything better to do. Bree and Savannah have already put their feet down about you two not sleeping together the night before your wedding, and apparently that means *all* of us need to spend the night apart from our wives due to some kind of sisterly solidarity."

Riley laughed. "I love my future sisters-in-law."

"We might have to break that torturous rule." Josh stole a kiss from her.

"It's bad luck to see the bride before the wedding," Riley said with knitted brows.

"That's an old wives' tale," Hugh said. "It's bad luck *not* to make love to your bride-to-be the night *before* your wedding."

"I'll buy into that." Josh brought Riley's hand to his lips and pressed a kiss to the back of it. "I have no interest in sleeping apart from you anytime. Especially not when we're at a romantic, secluded inn."

Chapter Two

THE DRIVE FROM the airstrip to the resort was a rough one. Thick branches arched over tire-rutted grass and dirt. Thankfully, Jack was used to navigating rarely traveled mountain roads. Not only was he a bush pilot, ex–Special Forces, and the director of a survival training program, but he and Savannah owned a remote cabin in these very mountains. Riley trusted him completely.

When the resort finally came into view, it was even more stunning than she remembered from their visit with Charlotte, the owner. Charlotte was an erotic-romance writer who had inherited the inn and had made it—or rather, one wing of it—her home. Hal had been close to Charlotte's parents, and he'd known Charlotte since she was born. Luckily, like everyone else who knew Hal, she adored him, and when he inquired about having their wedding there, she was happy to open her doors for it.

Riley leaned closer to the window to get a better look. Three gorgeous stories of glass, stone, and cedar with grand terraces overlooked the lake, sprawling meadows, and picturesque mountains. She loved everything about the Big Apple, save for the media vultures, but nothing compared to the crisp mountain air and the scenic views of Colorado. It never failed to surprise her how just being in Colorado for a few minutes could make her long for her small-town roots—and her best friend. As an only child, Jade had been like the sister Riley had never had growing up. And since she'd come together with Josh, his sister and sisters-in-law had also warmly brought her into their close-knit circle, creating more sisterly bonds than she could ever have hoped for. They didn't all live in Colorado, but they made time for family often—something she and Josh had missed out on a little too frequently lately due to work commitments. Yet another reason to move closer to home for at least part of the year.

"Jack," Riley said, stepping from the SUV. "I can't thank you and Hugh enough for getting us here." She hugged him. At well over six rugged feet, Jack, like Josh's brother Rex, was built like a lumberjack, with impossibly wide shoulders, bulbous muscles sprouting on top of muscles, and thick, powerful legs. She preferred her fiancé's sleeker, perfectly defined body. Josh kept in prime shape through running rather than hard physical labor, like Jack and Rex. But she knew their wives loved their physiques just as much as she loved Josh's.

"Anything for you guys." Jack opened the trunk of the SUV, grabbed a duffel bag, and tossed it to Hugh, then hoisted a leather bag over his shoulder.

Josh and Riley's bags had been shipped to Rex and Jade weeks earlier so as not to call any attention to their plan, along with the wedding dress she and Josh had designed together.

"Besides, it gave me and Hugh a chance to pick up a few things for our kids while we were in the Bahamas. What did you pick up?" Jack nodded to the box she was carrying.

"Elisabeth made me brownies." Elisabeth was Josh's cousin

Ross's fiancée. She and Ross were getting married this weekend in the Bahamas. Elisabeth owned a mobile bakery in Trusty, Colorado, and everything she baked was delicious.

"That box doesn't look nearly big enough for all the girls and the kids, and I'm not sure Bree will want Christian hopped up on brownies while the wedding preparations are taking place. You know how hyper he gets." Hugh held out a hand with a glint of mischief in his eyes. "I'll take care of them for you."

Riley clutched the box against her chest. "Not a chance, buster. But you have a good point. It would be hard to tell any of the kids they can't have some."

Josh shrugged off his jacket and wrapped it around the box. "I'll put it in our room for you and the girls."

"Best fiancé ever!" Riley went up on her toes and kissed him.

As they headed inside, Riley felt her stress falling away. There was no more running, no more hiding or hoping their secret wedding didn't get leaked to the press. Except, of course, their secret baby news. Keeping her excitement hidden from Jade was killing her. But every time they spoke, Jade raved about her new baby boy, and Riley couldn't bring herself to dampen Jade's excitement with worry over her own situation. In another few weeks it would be safe for them to tell the world. She hoped and prayed every day that her confused womb was no longer befuddled and had settled into nurturing their tiny miracle.

Riley's parents were arriving later that afternoon, and the wedding was scheduled for tomorrow evening on the terrace overlooking the lake. In order to keep their big day under wraps, they'd decided to do everything themselves, from making the food and wedding cake to the dresses and decorations. Riley had taken private baking and cake decorating lessons from her friend Molly, a baker who lived around the corner from their apartment in New York City. Molly owned a catering business, and in addition to teaching her how to make the cake, she'd lent Riley all the accouterments she'd need to make a beautiful wedding cake. With the help of Josh's family, they should have plenty of time to make their homespun wedding everything they'd dreamed of.

Inside the resort they were met with a sweet, woody scent, which was both comforting and homey, despite the immensity of the property. High ceilings with exposed beams boasted antler and iron chandeliers. Riley took in the worn hardwood floors and stone walls, wondering what secrets they held. Had Josh's mother stood in this very spot all those years ago, as nervous as Riley was about her wedding coming together? Or had she been too overwhelmed with love to worry at all? She'd heard so many stories from Josh's family about his mother, it was as if she still walked among them.

Josh gathered her in his arms. "It's perfect, isn't it, baby?"

"I can't imagine anyplace better."

"Oh my gosh! You're here!" Max's hushed but excited voice drew them apart. Her efficient ponytail swung behind her as she hurried across the floor in her jeans and T-shirt and threw her arms around Riley. "I was afraid someone would spot you leaving and you'd end up rerouting to someplace else." She stepped back and ran her eyes down Riley's body. "Only you could glow like that after the night you've had. Wait until Jade sees you! She's upstairs getting baby Hal—I mean *little Hal*, dressed."

"Thanks, Max. I can't wait to see everyone." Her eyes swept over Max's pretty face. "You look different. Gorgeous, as always, but different."

"Contacts," Max said with a shrug. "I got tired of Jade begging me to try them, and I finally gave in."

Riley's bestie had a way of making people do things. Jade could probably convince Riley to fly if she tried hard enough.

Josh embraced Max. "Thanks for helping us out this weekend."

"Do you really think you need to thank me? You guys are finally getting married!" Max covered her mouth. "Oops. Kids are still sleeping. We'd better be quiet."

"Well, as always, you look hot," Riley said. "And Jade can be a little pushy."

"I am *not* pushy. I'm *convincing*." Jade strutted down the wide staircase with her little raven-haired baby boy on her hip. He was the spitting image of his brooding father, from his serious dark eyes right down to the tiny jeans and dark T-shirt he wore.

Riley reached for the baby. "Give me that handsome little devil. I've missed baby Hal."

"I have a baby and suddenly I'm unworthy of a hello?" Jade handed over her adorable little boy. Her black hair was pulled back in a clip, probably to keep it away from her baby's grabby hands. "And by the way, right now he's 'little Hal.' But you know how my macho Rexy is. In another month he'll be calling him 'big Hal.'"

"He'll always be 'baby Hal' to me, but I guess I can get used to 'little Hal.' And I can't wait to get my hands on Finn, too." She smiled down at the baby, tamping down the urge to reveal her big news. Josh's brother Dane and his wife, Lacy's, son, Finn, was a few weeks older than little Hal. Riley nuzzled against little Hal's pudgy cheeks, making him giggle. The sound was music to her ears. He was almost a year old, but he still had that unique baby scent that tugged at all her maternal strings. "Little Hal and Finn are going to be trouble when they're older."

"Only half as much trouble as Christian and Dylan," Hugh said. Dylan was Treat and Max's son. Hugh pulled Jade into an embrace and gave her a loud kiss on her cheek. "You look beautiful. Now, where's my hot wife?"

"*Roar*," Jade teased as Jack drew her into a quick hug. "She's upstairs helping Layla pick out an outfit for Christian. Layla is quite the attentive sister."

"That's my girl." Hugh took the steps two at a time.

Riley soaked in the ever-present affection of Josh's family. They embraced and watched over each other's wives and children as if they were their own, and she felt like the luckiest girl in the world to be marrying into such a loving family.

"Is Savannah upstairs with Adam?" Jack asked, heading for the stairs to see his wife and baby.

"No." Max pointed toward the rear of the house. "Finn's teething. He was up three times last night. She and Lacy are taking a walk with the babies out back. And Hal's walking the property with Treat, Dane, and Rex, probably making lists of repairs that need to be done to the inn."

"Josh, you might as well go outside with the men," Jade suggested. "Because I'm stealing your fiancée to go over wedding preparations. It's my right as matron of honor."

Josh feigned a growl and leaned toward Riley for a kiss. "I'll take your goodies up to our room, and then I'll join them outside." He held up the box of brownies still wrapped in his jacket.

"It's okay. I've got it." Riley took the box. "Go have fun

with your family. Love you."

He stole another kiss. "Love you, too, babe. And no worrying."

Riley snuggled little Hal as she watched Josh walk away. His white shirt fit his broad back and slim waist to mouthwatering perfection and disappeared into a pair of dark jeans that hugged his butt perfectly.

"Don't drool on my baby." Jade took little Hal from her. "I swear our Braden men have us wrapped around their little fingers, don't they?"

Riley arched a brow. "I assure you, there's nothing *little* about my man."

"Oh Lord. Here we go." Max rolled her eyes. "Before we go down the 'my man's meat is bigger than yours' path, what are you worried about? The wedding?"

"A little. And we've been talking about where we want to live when we start our family," Riley confessed. "But let's not talk about that right now. I want to think about things I know the answers to, like how fantastic our wedding is going to be."

"Don't you mean how fantastic your wedding *night* is going to be?" Jade waggled her brows.

They giggled their way into the kitchen, where they found Charlotte standing in front of the griddle wearing a pair of skimpy denim shorts and a man's button-down shirt that was at least two sizes too big, rolled up at the cuffs and unbuttoned three buttons deep. Her head was cocked to the side, and she was scribbling in a notebook with one hand while holding a spatula with the other and...moaning.

Sensually.

Max grabbed Jade's and Riley's arms, stopping them from going any closer.

Charlotte's head lolled back, eyes closed, and she let out a breathy sigh. Riley bit back a giggle. Charlotte's back arched, and she moaned again. Her hips rocked forward, and her hand—the one with the spatula—dragged down her thigh as another needy sound escaped her lips. It was like watching a one-sided pornographic cooking show. Suddenly she leaned forward, her dark hair curtaining her face, and she scribbled something in the notebook again.

"Um...I want whatever you had for breakfast!" Riley said with a laugh.

Charlotte squealed. "You're here!" Her cheeks were flushed, like she'd just had sex. She shoved the pen behind her ear and looked at the spatula and then at the griddle, as if she wasn't sure what to do with either.

"Here, give it to me, Char. You're dangerous with cooking utensils." Max took the spatula and gave her a friendly shove toward Riley.

"Thanks for letting us barge in on, uh, whatever *that* was." Riley hugged her with one hand, still holding the box of brownies in the other. They had met only a few times, but they'd instantly clicked despite Charlotte's inability to focus on anything other than writing for longer than a few minutes due to a publishing deadline. Riley and Josh had assured her they would handle everything for the wedding and not interrupt her work.

"I feel like I need a cigarette," Jade joked.

"The life of an erotic-romance writer is never dull." Charlotte tickled little Hal's belly. "Then again, I guess your mama's life is never dull either, is it, cutie pie? I'd like one of these little guys of my own one day. But the closest I come to baby making is inked on the pages of my books. I'm so glad you guys are here. It's nice to hear some life in this big old place."

"Oh my gosh. Charlotte!" Max exclaimed, staring down at the griddle. She lowered her voice and said, "Penis pancakes?"

Riley and Jade sidled up to Max to check them out. Sure enough, in the pan were two pancakes, each around eight inches long and two inches thick, complete with bulbous mushroom caps and roundish testicles.

"Research." Charlotte was one of those women who didn't walk; she moved like she was either on a mission or completely lost. There was no in between. Clearly on a mission, she took the spatula from Max and flipped the pancakes. "What do you think? Pretty lifelike, right?" She set the spatula beside the stove and picked up her notebook. "I'm writing a story about a grocery store clerk who hooks up with an erotic male dancer. She's a nightmare in the kitchen, which I can totally relate to, but she can cook pancakes. Like...*only* pancakes. After they hook up, she makes him dinner." She eyed the pancakes again. "I think it totally works, right?"

"Lord," Max said under her breath.

Jade peered at the griddle again. "Looks about an inch too small, and too thin. Definitely too thin."

Riley laughed. "No comment. I wouldn't want to make you feel like you were missing out." Jade elbowed her, and they roared with laughter.

"They're going to burn." Max snagged the spatula and flipped them again. "I can't believe I'm flipping a penis."

"That would be penises," Jade offered.

"Or peni?" Riley suggested. "What's the plural of it anyway?"

"Cocks? Schlongs? Flesh P—" Jade bent over in hysterics. "Flesh Popsicles?"

Max turned beet-red. "You are so *bad*."

"Oh, come on. It took me forever to get them right." Charlotte grabbed a plate from the other side of the counter and set it in front of them. It was piled high with crooked penis pancakes.

"This one looks like the Leaning Tower of Pisa," Jade pointed out.

"Why do you have to make them and get them right? They're not actually going *in* the book." Riley gasped. "Oh my gosh. Char, do you do *all* your research hands-on? For *everything?*"

All eyes turned to Charlotte, who seemed unaffected by their curiosity and delighted at the prospect of researching erotic love scenes with their men. "Well, sure." She tucked a wayward lock of her tousled dark hair behind her ear. "I mean, if I'm going to write about a couple having sex on the stairs, I have to make sure the angle works, right? And it's not just the size and shape of the pancake that matters for research. It's the *making* of it. I have to imagine a man nibbling my neck while I'm stirring, or flipping, or—"

"*Coming*," Jade suggested.

Max's cheeks burned redder. "Jade!"

"Best. Job. Ever," Riley added. "So, who's the lucky research partner? Some hunky mountain man?"

Char scoffed. "You're kidding, right? You think there are men around here? Nope. Just me and my blow-up dolls. It's the mechanics of the scenes that need to work, not the…"

"Intensity of the orgasms?" Jade asked. "Because I think that's what really matters. And we are *so* going to fix your no-man problem," Jade promised.

Charlotte shook her head. "I'm not the dating type, but

thank you very much. Guys are a pain. They get jealous of my hours at the keyboard, and they're never as attentive as the heroes I create. It's a recipe for disaster."

"Funny," Riley said. "I'm never disappointed with Josh in the attentiveness department. Maybe you're just going out with the wrong guys."

"Whatever." Charlotte waved a hand dismissively.

"You know," Max said. "Our hubbies have all those single cousins out in Pleasant Hill, Maryland. I bet Beau Braden could help you fix this place right up. He's smart and funny, not to mention handsome—"

"Thanks," Charlotte said, cutting her off. "But he's a man, which means he'll be jealous and demanding, and like I said, not nearly as *good* as my heroes. Better to live in a fantasy world that I can turn on and off with the flick of a switch."

"Or an air pump," Jade added.

Charlotte laughed. "I'm never naked with my dolls. Gosh, you guys should write dirty books." She picked up a pancake from the plate and bit the head off of one of the crooked penises. "A dirty mind is a wonderful thing."

"I smell pancakes!" Max and Treat's daughter, Adriana, said as she bounded into the kitchen with her younger brother, Dylan, putting an end to their matchmaking efforts and penis talk.

"Incoming!" Jade moved between the griddle and the kids.

Riley put the box of brownies on top of the fridge before the kids could ask about it.

"Aunt Riley!" Adriana threw her arms around Riley's waist. At almost seven she was tall and lanky, with eyes as green as the grandmother she was named after and hair as thick as Max's and as dark as Treat's.

"I want some!" Dylan stretched to his tiptoes to peer above the edge of the counter. He, too, was tall, but at just shy of four years old, he was still not quite tall enough.

Thank goodness.

Max pushed the plate of pancakes away from her son's eager hands. "Those are Charlotte's pancakes. I'll make you some of your own."

"They can eat the pancakes. I've already set the scene in my head." Charlotte grabbed a plate from the cabinet, oblivious to Max's glare. She took a fork and knife from the drawer, cut off the pancake testicles, rearranged them on the plate, and handed it to Dylan. "A rocket ship and two clouds." She winked at Max and whispered, "Writers are very creative."

Guess she isn't oblivious after all.

"May I please have a rocket ship?" Adriana asked so politely Riley's heart squeezed.

"Let the morning madness begin," Jade said excitedly. "Big rockets for everyone! Can we make some with *smoke* coming out of the top?"

"Yeah!" the kids screamed.

Riley tried to squelch a laugh and snorted, earning a round of laughter from everyone else.

Max shook her head. "See what you're missing by living in New York, Ri? Jade and the kids and I have breakfast together several times a week. I *know* what Jade's breakfast special will be from now on."

"Rocket ships and…" Jade's eyes sparked with mischief. "Twin mountain peaks." She and Riley laughed again.

"My job here is done," Charlotte said with a satisfied smirk. "Back to my writing."

"Just a sec," Max said. "Last night Rex and Treat noticed

that some of the railings were loose on the terrace where we're going to have the ceremony. Since they're building the canopy, they said they could fix those, too, but they couldn't find the wood they had delivered last month."

"Oh, right. Sorry. It's in the woodshed down by Snow White's cabin."

Max arched a brow.

"Sorry. The original log cabin. If you saw it, you'd understand. When I was younger, I expected dwarfs to come out whistling every time I went down there. Too bad I never saw the handsome prince. I'll draw you a map." Charlotte tore a piece of paper from her notebook and began drawing a map. "There's a small tractor and trailer in the shed they can use to transport the wood. At least there was when I first moved in. I haven't been out there for three years."

"Three *years*?" Max asked.

"Yeah. I wasn't kidding when I said I never leave my little wing of this place. I only opened this big kitchen for you guys a few days ago. And I didn't get everything cleaned out. So I'd stay away from the cabinets on that end of the room." Charlotte waved her hand toward the intricately detailed maple cabinets across the enormous kitchen. "I live on microwaved foods, peanut butter and jam, and energy bars. I usually use my kitchenette, but I didn't want to miss welcoming Josh and Riley this morning." She handed the paper to Max.

"What are these?" Max pointed to several points on the map.

"Rock formations, groups of trees. You'll know when you get there," Charlotte assured her.

"Why don't you open the resort again?" Riley asked. "I bet you could make a killing."

Charlotte shrugged. "Maybe one day, but right now I'm perfectly happy writing. Besides, there's a ton of work to be done around here. The railings are only the tip of the iceberg, and I don't have time to breathe." She tousled Dylan's hair. "Enjoy the pancakes, little man. You girls can come get me if you need anything—but you might want to knock first." She winked and headed out of the kitchen.

"Hi, Char," Brianna said, passing Charlotte on her way out of the kitchen as she entered with Layla and Christian.

Layla made a beeline for Riley, giving her big hug. "Hi, Aunt Riley. Mommy said Adriana and I can make the flower headdresses for the wedding. We found some pretty flowers by the lake. I can't wait to make them."

"Layla!" Adriana smiled brightly, patting the chair beside her. "Sit with me."

Layla settled in beside her.

Riley could hardly believe how big the girls had gotten. They leaned in close, whispering and giggling just like she and Jade had always done. She hoped her baby would have a bestie she or he adored, too.

A few minutes later Savannah came through the door with Adam in her arms. At just over a year old, Adam was the spitting image of his father, Jack. Lacy followed her in, carrying Finn, who was almost a year old, as blond as she was, and as dark-eyed as Dane.

Christian and Dylan were all giggles and blast-off noises as they gobbled down pancakes at the table, while Jade and the other women joked about *rocket ships* and *explosions*. Riley soaked it all in. She gazed out the window at Josh, who was talking with Dane and Hal beneath the leafy umbrella of a large tree. Treat, Hugh, and Jack stood a few feet away, and in the distance, Rex was leading Hope toward them. She loved that Hal had brought Hope to the wedding. Hope was as much a part of their family as any of them. She wished Josh's mother could see her beautiful family coming together to help prepare for their special day.

"Let's go over the plans for today." Max set a notebook on the counter beside Riley and began ticking off their to-do list. Although Jade was the matron of honor, everyone knew Max was the best organizer on the planet. Jade had worked with her to make all the arrangements, but with her new baby boy to care for, she was happy to let Max do what she did best. The men were in charge of building the canopy, fixing the railings, stringing lights, and making sure the terrace was baby-proofed.

"Hal offered to help keep the kids busy making wedding decorations while we cook and make your wedding cake," Jade added.

"I saw all the cake pans. Your friend Molly really came through for you," Savannah said, repositioning Adam on her hip. He clung to a fistful of her hair like a security blanket.

"Molly is awesome. And Josh is going to be so surprised. He thinks we're doing a fancy sheet cake, not a four-tier real wedding cake." Riley smiled, thinking about the day she had surprised Josh with the news of their pregnancy. They'd both gotten teary-eyed imagining what life would be like with midnight feedings, a crib in a nursery, and baby toys strewn about the living room.

Brianna set another pancake on Christian's plate. "Last one, piglet." She kissed him on the top of his head.

"Aw, Mom," he complained around a mouthful of pancake.

"I swear he'd eat until there was no more food if we let him." Brianna pushed her dark hair behind her ear and reached for Finn. "I'm feeling the urge for another baby. Maybe Finny will scratch that itch."

"Why not let Hugh scratch it?" Savannah bounced Adam on her hip. Eyeing the children, she lowered her voice and said, "We're thinking about trying for another. I want Adam to be close to his siblings."

"Besides," Lacy whispered, "trying is *so* much fun." She'd secured her blond corkscrew curls at the nape of her neck with a blue clip that matched her eyes. "We're not *trying* to get pregnant, but we aren't *not* trying either." Her eyes danced with excitement. "No bun in the oven so far, but maybe next month we'll get lucky."

"How about you, Ri?" Jade asked. "You said you guys were going to try right away."

Riley's confession was on the tip of her tongue, but she had another few weeks before she'd feel like she was out of the woods. The last thing she wanted was to make her friends worry about her pregnancy when they were in such high spirits. Not wanting to outright lie, she said, "I went off the pill."

"You did?" Jade asked. "How did I not know that?"

"It's not like she needed to ask your permission," Savannah joked.

Jade looked at Riley, her eyes suddenly a little sad. "No, but there was a time when we knew everything about each other."

Riley's heart ached. There was a time when Jade would have been the first person she'd told about such a big decision. But their lives were busier now, and their priorities had shifted. Jade was married with a new baby, and Riley's life had become one deadline after another. While she and Jade used to talk on the phone at least four times each week, they now texted only a few times a week. And the night Riley and Josh had made the decision that Riley would stop taking birth control was *their* monumental moment. Wasn't that the way their lives were supposed to evolve? To mold and shape around the people they grew to love as much—or more than—their very best friend?

"It's only a matter of time before we'll be throwing you a baby shower, Ri," Max said excitedly. "Maybe a triple one with Lacy and Savannah. How fun would that be?"

Before Riley could answer, Jade reached for her hand. "Maybe you'll get pregnant right away. Our babies could be in the same classes and grow up as close as we are."

Riley's heartbeat sped up, and she had to fight hard not to tell Jade her news. But she and Josh had made a joint decision, and she'd never betray him like that.

"I hope so." Her honest confession sparked a litany of hopeful comments.

Surrounded by sweet baby noises, happy whispers, and the warmth of family, Riley let her hand drift to her belly as she gazed out the window again, her eyes immediately finding her handsome fiancé. Josh turned, scanning the windows as if he felt her gaze on him. Their eyes locked, the electricity between them as hot as ever and the love carrying it as real and stable as the mountains they stood upon.

JOSH AND HIS brothers stood in the yard discussing the work that needed to be completed for the wedding. As Rex looked over the map Charlotte had drawn, which would guide them to the woodshed, Josh thought about the other things that needed to be done. Once they found the woodshed, building the canopy would be time-consuming but definitely doable. Rex and Jack were experts at building things. Fixing the railings and stringing lights around the terrace were a piece of cake, but making sure the terrace was completely baby-proofed? Josh didn't know the first thing about baby-proofing, but it was about time he learned. First, though, they had to find the woodshed.

"Are you kidding me?" Rex stared at the map with an annoyed look on his face.

"It can't be that bad." Jack took the map from him and chuckled. "Okay, maybe it can be that bad. Heart tree? What's a heart tree?"

Hal cleared his throat and reached up to pet Hope.

Treat snagged the map from Jack. At six foot six, he stood shoulder to shoulder with their father and had a solid few inches over each of his siblings. "Max would never let these directions pass without asking for an explanation." He studied the map. "Snow White's house? This is like a fairy-tale wild-goose chase. I have a feeling someone's pulling our legs. Hold on. Let me check."

Hal put an arm around Josh's shoulder and leaned in close. "Your mother would get a kick out of this."

"At her sons being totally perplexed?" Josh asked.

Hal shrugged. "She'd never ask for directions. She'd take that map and follow it to a tee, just to see what she could discover along the way."

Treat pulled out his cell phone and called Max. "Sweetness, we're having some trouble with these directions." He paused, his brows lifted, and a small smile slid across his face. "Sounds good. Thanks, beautiful. How're the kids? Okay. Absolutely. Put her on." He lowered the mouthpiece and said, "Adriana wants to say something. Hold on." As he listened again, his smile widened. "Okay, precious girl. I'll let him know. Yes. Yes. Okay, love you, sweetheart."

"Well?" Rex crossed his arms, his biceps twitching with impatience as Treat put his phone in his pocket.

"Adriana wants Hugh to know that Dylan wants a race car for Christmas," Treat explained.

"That's a boy after my own heart," Hugh said. "Christian's already got a little go-kart. I can have one made for Dylan."

"Adriana also said she doesn't want you to buy him one, because they're too dangerous." Treat put a hand on Hugh's shoulder. "So before you go having anything made, I suggest you take it up with Max and Adriana. You're liable to get an earful."

"Come on, bro," Hugh said. "Go-karts are a rite of passage."

"Then you'll have no issue with me teaching Christian to dive with sharks when he's older?" Dane gave Treat an I've-got-your-back nod.

"That's totally different," Hugh argued. "You can't control a shark."

"Like you can control a race car?" Dane scoffed. "Give me a break."

"We're talking about go-karts, not race cars," Hugh pointed out. "And why are you so persnickety? You drove them when we were young. Like I said, it's a rite of passage."

"There are no *rites of passage* once you're married," Jack reminded them. "Joint decisions, concessions. That's the name of the happily-ever-after game."

"Thank God Riley and I have the same beliefs about kids," Josh said under his breath.

"That won't matter," Hugh said. "You could have a kid who wants to follow in my footsteps, or Treat's, or Rex's, or he could swim with sharks like Dane. You can't control what kids want."

"No, but I can control what I allow them to do," Josh responded.

"All I know is, my boy's never going anywhere near sharks or race cars," Rex said. "He can sit his ass on a tractor or a horse. Can we focus now? Christ, Josh will never get married if we dick around all day. Treat, what did Max say about the map?"

"Apparently Charlotte told her we'd understand each landmark when we got there." He shrugged. "We have a lot to get done. I suggest we split up."

"Rex," Hal said, his deep voice commanding all of their attention. "Why don't you come with me and Josh to the woodshed. Dane and Hugh, string the lights. Treat and Jack, you're on railing duty. Check the railings on all the terraces, not just this one. Always leave a place better than you found it. And when we get back, we can get started building the frame for the canopy and try to figure out what the heck is involved with baby-proofing the terrace."

Treat nodded toward the others. "You heard the man. Let's go." He patted their father on the back. "You sure you're okay trekking through the woods?"

It was no secret that Hal was still desperately in love with, Adriana, or that he believed he communicated with her through Hope. A few years ago he'd been hospitalized with heart-attack-like symptoms and had been diagnosed with broken heart syndrome, the symptoms of which mirrored those of a heart attack. They'd been as relieved as they were distressed by his diagnosis and had watched him a little closer ever since.

"Son, your mother and I spent so much time in these woods

together I could navigate them blindfolded. When the day comes that I can no longer walk a trail, then you'll be putting me six feet under. Until then, have faith that your old man can handle just about anything."

"Hold up a sec," Rex said with a pinched look on his face. "If you know the property that well, then you know how to get to the woodshed. Why didn't you say something?"

Hal laughed. "Because your mother always loved watching you boys run in circles." He strode forward and motioned for Rex and Josh to follow. "Let's go, before the women come out here wondering why we're slacking off."

The scent of pine hung in the air as Josh followed his father through the woods, weaving around tall trees and spiny bushes. Twigs crunched beneath their feet, reminding him of his youth, when he and his siblings traipsed all over their family's property.

Rex elbowed Josh and hiked a thumb over his shoulder just as Hope's big body ambled around a tree. They both laughed. Hope had a way of sneaking up on them.

"You sure you don't want to put her in the pasture by the barn?" Josh suggested.

His brother lifted his chin toward their father's broad back. "He said she knows these parts as well as he does." He arched a thick black brow. "Guess he was right." They walked in silence for a beat, and then Rex asked, "You nervous?"

"About getting married? Not really. I just want everything to go smoothly so Riley gets the wedding day she's always dreamed of. It's bad enough that we have to hide out to get it."

"She won't," Rex said with a serious tone. "No one gets a perfect wedding, except maybe Treat. I swear that man has the luck of the Irish. Hell, Jade and I got married in a hospital. There's no way you'll beat that. You'll either get married on the terrace or inside a gorgeous resort. It won't matter either way, because Riley will become your wife, and the moment that happens, it'll outshine anything that goes wrong."

Hope *neigh*ed, causing them both to smile.

Hal was quiet as they made their way through the long grass. They followed him around a large grouping of rocks to a steep hillside.

"Whoa, girl." Rex reached his arm out behind them, stopping Hope from getting too close to the edge.

Hope stopped walking and pushed her head against the center of his chest. He stroked a hand over her cheek. "That's a girl."

Josh joined his father by the craggy outcropping. A bushy formation of gnarled and twisted trunks of a limber pine tree grew at an impressive angle, as if powerful winds were blowing it over the edge and it refused to fall. Branches stretched like knobby, aged hands tipped with spiky green needles.

Hal squinted against the sun, gazing out over the valley below. "This was one of your mother's favorite spots."

Rex stepped beside Josh, keeping one eye on Hope, who appeared happy to hang back beneath the cover of the trees. "It sure is beautiful."

"So was your mother." Hal lifted his chin toward the limber pine, a mannerism that Rex had honed so well, Josh saw his brother in the motion.

His father's sun-kissed cheeks had a few more deep grooves than Josh remembered. A breeze caught Hal's thick hair, and Josh noticed it had become more silver than black. It was easy for him to see his father as the strong man he'd always been and it was painful to acknowledge the harsh reality. Despite his outward size and strength from continuing to work the ranch, his father was aging. He was glad he and Riley were considering moving back to Weston. He'd like as much time with his father as he could get.

"This is the heart tree," Hal said with pride in his eyes. "Your mother wanted to leave her mark everywhere we went. When Charlotte was little she used to call this the heart tree, and I guess it stuck."

Josh scanned the tree again, and slowly an etched heart came into focus where two of the trunks had grown together, covering the upper-right arch of the carved heart. Inside the deeply grooved symbol of his parents' love were their initials, with a plus sign between them. After everything he'd been told about his mother, and the pictures he'd seen of his parents, it was easy for him to imagine the two of them in this very spot.

"I wish she was here now," Josh said honestly. "For you, Dad, as much as for me." They'd never really talked about his mother's passing, and the question Josh had been silencing for years rose to the surface. For the first time in his life, he didn't try to quell the ache it carried or suppress his desire for answers.

Rex huffed out a breath, crossed his arms, and shifted his eyes over the ridge.

"Don't worry, son," his father said. "She's always with me."

"Do you think she knew?" Forcing the words from his lungs was harder than he anticipated. "You always talk about how Mom was spiritual and how she's still around. But do you think she knew her life would be cut short?"

"Can we change the subject?" Rex grumbled.

"Sorry, Rex. I know you don't like to talk about this stuff, but you *knew* her. I never did, and I'm left...I don't know...trying to fill in the gaps, I guess."

Rex ground his teeth together. "Point me in the direction of the woodshed. I'll go get started while you two reminisce."

"Re—"

Hal grabbed Josh's arm and shook his head. "Rex, head south until the roof comes into view and then cut left around the conifers. You'll find the way. Hope'll get you there."

"Christ," Rex said under his breath. He patted his thigh and made a clicking sound through clenched teeth, as if he were calling a dog. Hope ambled forward, and Rex mounted her. "I'll see you two down there."

"I didn't mean to make him uncomfortable," Josh apologized.

"You didn't make him uncomfortable. Talking about your mother makes his mind go places he doesn't want to be taken. That boy loves Jade and little Hal more than life itself. Thinking of your mother makes him think of losing them." Hal put an arm around Josh's shoulder and walked in the direction Rex had gone.

"If this is too tough for you to talk about, we don't have to," Josh offered.

"Talking about your mother is never tough. Her face is still the first thing I see when I wake up, and at the end of a long day, it's the image I see when I close my eyes."

"Don't you get lonely, Dad?" For some reason, he'd been wondering about that a lot lately.

"Lonely?" Hal's hearty laughter sailed around them. "I had six young 'uns to raise, and then each of you brought me a son or daughter-in-law to love like my own flesh and blood. And now we've been blessed with beautiful grandchildren. Son, there is no room for loneliness in my life, and that's probably exactly what your mother had planned all along."

Josh looked at his father skeptically. "So you *do* think she knew?"

Hal shook his head. "No, Josh. She couldn't have…" He paused, his brows knitted, as if he were thinking over his response. A long moment later he said, "All I know is that my darlin' girl is smiling down at us happy as a lark that our family has remained so close."

Josh believed that with his whole heart.

A rustic, Tudor-style cottage came into view, and sure enough, it looked just like Snow White's cottage with duo A-line roofs that sloped nearly to the ground and an arched door made of barn wood.

"Before we were married, your mother and I would come up to see our friends—Charlotte's parents—and this is where we stayed. In separate rooms, of course," he said with a smirk.

Josh couldn't decipher that smirk and he wasn't about to ask. He hoped his parents had taken advantage of every second they'd had together. Just like he intended to do with Riley. And as they headed to the woodshed just beyond the house, where Rex was loading up a small trailer, Hope came into view, and Josh swore her eyes shone a little brighter.

Chapter Three

THE KITCHEN SMELLED heavenly. Riley and the girls had been baking and preparing for tomorrow's big event all afternoon. Four layers of white wedding cake sat cooling on the counter, their sweet aroma tempting Riley with every breath as she and Brianna dipped strawberries in chocolate. The chocolate ganache was perfectly prepared (they'd tasted it several times, just to be sure), and cooling in a big bowl covered with plastic wrap. Jade was cutting vegetables for kabobs, and Savannah and Lacy were using cookie cutters to cut fruit for a decorative fruit salad. Country music and Top 40 songs streamed from Jade's iPhone while they danced and sang their way around the kitchen with two little ones who were eager to help underfoot.

"Please lemme stir!" Christian tugged on the hem of Max's shirt as she mixed the homemade marinade for tomorrow's steaks. She was using one of Josh's mother's recipes, which Savannah had dug out of her mother's old recipe cards.

"It's my turn," Dylan reminded him. "You stirred last time."

"You both may have one last turn." Max stood between the two boys, both of whom were now climbing onto chairs beside her.

Riley looked up from the strawberry she was dipping in chocolate and glanced out the window. "Looks like Grandpa Hal is on his way in."

"Yay!" Dylan and Christian exclaimed in unison as they scrambled off the chairs and scurried toward the door to greet their grandfather.

Max laughed. "Well, I guess we know where their priorities lie."

Finn's cry sounded through the baby monitor, and Lacy sighed. She'd just put him down twenty minutes earlier. "My poor boy. Doesn't anyone have a good remedy for teething?"

"Brandy," Brianna offered. She dipped a strawberry in the vat of chocolate and set it on wax paper to cool. "Not that I've tried it, but that's what everyone always told me."

"Hm." Lacy's blue eyes lit up. "Liquor the kid up. That sounds like a great idea…if I were a horrible mother."

They all laughed.

"I think she meant *you* could use the brandy," Jade suggested.

"I have wine." Lacy took a sip from her glass, then set it on the counter and headed for the stairs. "But I still feel bad for my little man."

Hal came through the door and scooped one young boy up in each arm. "Let's go, you little rascals."

"Dad, you shouldn't be carrying them," Savannah chided him.

"Nonsense." He carried the giggling boys into the living room, where Brianna and Max had set out toys, markers, crayons, and the cardboard stars the girls had cut out to be strung as decorations.

"Mommy, can Adriana and I ask Daddy to help us make

the headdresses now?" Layla asked.

"He's working on the terrace, honey," Brianna answered. "They'll come get you when they're ready."

"I'll take them." Savannah set a star-shaped piece of honeydew melon on a platter and lifted Adam from the high chair onto her hip. "We could use a little fresh air before I start gobbling down those strawberries."

"Start?" Riley cocked a brow. They'd each already eaten several of the sweet treats. She'd be surprised if any were left for the wedding. Her phone rang, and she wiped her hands before reaching for it.

"Saved by the bell," Savannah said, then turned to the girls, speaking in a conspiratorial whisper. "Come on, girls, let's grab one more strawberry before Auntie Riley gets off the phone."

Giggling, they each grabbed a strawberry and hurried out the door.

"Honey," Riley's mother said through the phone. "Are you there?"

"Yes, sorry, Mom. It's a little busy around here. Where are you? I thought you'd be here by now." Her parents should have arrived an hour ago.

"I'm sorry, but your father and I are running late. We'll be there sometime after dinner."

"After *dinner?*" Her heart squeezed, and she told herself it was no big deal, but she missed her parents, and this was a big weekend for her. "I was really looking forward to spending today with you."

"I was, too, honey. But your father and I..." Her voice faded, and she cleared her throat. "We had some things to take care of. We didn't expect it to take this long. We'll be there as soon as we can."

Riley sighed. "Okay, but is everything all right?"

"Mm-hm. Fine. Don't worry about us. We'll see you soon."

"Mom, are you sure? Is something wrong with Daddy? You sound funny." She watched Jade pass by on her way into the living room.

"No, honey. He's fine," her mother assured her. "We just didn't sleep well last night, and had a hard time getting going this morning. We'll be there in a few hours. I love you, honey. Enjoy the girls, and I can't wait to see you."

They talked for a few more minutes, and by the time they hung up, Riley's mother had almost convinced her they were fine.

Almost.

It wasn't like her mother to miss such a big event. Thinking about the call, Riley wandered into the living room. Jade handed little Hal to his grandfather and gave her baby a kiss on the cheek. She looked happy and beautiful in a pair of cutoffs and cowgirl boots. She hadn't changed one bit since she was nineteen. Except she looked even happier now, which Riley had never thought possible, because Jade was a firecracker and her spark never dimmed.

"You sure you don't mind?" Jade glanced at Dylan and Christian, who were coloring the stars the girls had cut out as decorations. "You've already got these two goofballs to look after."

The boys giggled.

Hal pressed a kiss to the baby's forehead. "Darlin', this is half as many as I raised."

"Okay, well, holler if you need us." Jade headed back the way she'd come, and when her eyes met Riley's, her expression turned serious. "Uh-oh. What's wrong?"

"Nothing."

Jade settled her hands on her hips and scowled. "Riley Banks, you tell me what's going on, or I swear…"

Riley arched a brow. "Swear what?"

"Aw, heck. I've got nothing." Jade laughed and took Riley's hand, dragging her through the living room toward the study. "Let's check on your dress. That should bring a big smile to your pretty face."

Riley stumbled to keep up. "Why did you hang it down here?"

"Well, duh. You don't want to traipse down all those stairs, trip on your train, and fall on your ass tomorrow, do you?"

"No! I hadn't even considered that."

"You didn't need to. I'm the matron of honor. It's my job to make sure your nonfunctioning nervous-bride brain doesn't have to work too hard." Jade waved at the entrance to the study. Rich mahogany bookshelves lined the far wall, each shelf filled from end to end. A stone fireplace ran the full height of the wall to their left, flanked by two enormous windows overlooking the grounds.

Riley stepped into the room. Her wedding gown hung on a wooden coatrack that looked out of place in such a fine study. And just beyond, hanging from the back of a door that led to the dining room, were the girls' bridesmaid dresses.

Riley's heart skipped a beat, as it had every time she set her eyes on the gorgeous gown. She and Josh had designed and redesigned the dress time and time again, until every thread of lace in the halter bodice and every inch of the layered soft tulle skirt were perfect. They'd incorporated rose appliqué over the lace, reminiscent of the roses Josh had given her the night he proposed. Remembering the long hours they'd worked on it side by side, Riley thought, not for the first time, how they made perfect partners in every sense. Her hand moved to her belly, and her throat clogged with emotions. Jade must have felt the wave crashing over her, because she squeezed Riley's hand.

"It's stunning, Ri. I can feel the love you two put into the design."

Pressing her lips together hard to fend off another wave of emotions threatening to spill her secret, she nodded. Savannah came into the room and draped an arm over each of them.

"Where are the girls?" Jade asked.

"Treat is helping them make the headdresses like a pro. He said our mom showed him how." Savannah smirked. "Boy do I wish I knew that way back when. I could have teased him something awful. Now it's just the sweetest thing you've ever seen. That big man helping those adoring girls."

"And where's your little man?" Riley asked.

"He's with my dad, who is in his heyday with four boys to take care of. He'll have them working his ranch in no time."

Jade laughed. "Maybe we should let Finn and Adam sleep in his room tonight. See how much he misses it come morning, after getting up with them three times."

"Speaking of getting up at night, I checked on Lacy. She got Finn back to sleep, and she's conked out right beside him on the bed. I didn't think I should wake her."

"No, definitely let her sleep," Jade said. "The poor girl is probably exhausted."

Savannah ran her fingers over the knee-length bridesmaids' dresses. "These are so beautiful. And since each a little different, we can wear them again."

"Josh came up with the design for those." Riley was glad to have regained control of her emotions. "They're a modern twist on a classic dress." She pointed out the pleated, crossover bodice and A-line skirt. "The lines are perfect for curvy girls or skinny minnies. And the subtle beading along the neckline gives a nice little sparkle, don't you think?"

"Definitely." Jade turned Riley by the shoulders and gazed into her eyes with an understanding look Riley had seen for so many years, she could conjure it in her sleep. "Now, what happened with your mom?"

"How'd you know it was her on the phone?"

"Because everyone else who could make you look that worried is here with us."

"Did I miss something?" Savannah asked.

"Not really. My mom called. She said they didn't sleep well and they're running late."

"Oh, well, that's not bad, right?" Savannah asked.

Riley nodded. "But something in her voice sounded off."

"Or maybe that's the bride's nerves getting the best of her." Jade hugged her. "What do you say we get that cake ready before the kids get their hands on it?"

Twenty minutes later, with four round layers of wedding cake in varying sizes spread across the table, a bucket of premade white fondant at the ready, and five soon-to-be sisters-in-law standing elbow to elbow, eager to see weeks of practice in action, Riley reached for the bowl of ganache.

"What are the balls for?" Savannah pointed to a bowl of edible pearls.

"Decorations," Riley answered. "They're edible, and I thought we could create waves along the bottom of each layer."

"Aren't all balls edible?" Jade asked.

Riley laughed. Of course Jade would go there.

"Imagine how good they'll taste with the chocolate ganache

on them," Brianna exclaimed. "That chocolate's so good. I can't wait to get another taste!"

"On some balls?" Savannah tried to stifle a laugh, but it slipped out, causing the others to burst into laughter.

Brianna's cheeks flamed. "I didn't mean…"

"It's okay, Bree," Max said, giggling under her breath. "A little raunchiness is good for you. But you won't catch me talking about Treat's…*pearls*."

Riley doubled over in laughter. "Pearls! That reminds me. No pearl necklaces with the bridesmaid dresses!"

"Ohmygod." Max covered her face with her hands.

"Pearls? Rexy has baseballs," Jade said through fits of laughter. "Mm. Chocolate sexy Rexy ba—"

"Hey! Sister over here!" Savannah complained. "I do *not* need to think of my brother's—man parts."

Riley and Jade gulped air to try to quiet their laughter. "Sorry," they said in unison.

Riley busied herself unpeeling the plastic wrap and they all peered into the bowl.

"It looks perfect," Max declared.

They all exchanged a mischievous look, and at the same time, they each stuck a finger in the bowl and licked the chocolate off.

Max eyed Jade. "Don't. You. Dare."

Jade's eyes gleamed with mischief. "What?"

"You're going to say something about sucking or chocolate or both," Max said. "And don't double dip. No more fingers in the bowl."

"Yes, Mom," Savannah said.

Max rolled her eyes. "I'm just trying to keep the exchange of germs to a minimum."

"Whatever germs we have, we have already shared," Riley pointed out.

Max stuck her finger in the bowl again with a grin.

Jade glared at her.

"What?" Max said. "If you can't beat them…"

"Nothing." Jade grabbed a spoon and filled it with ganache.

"Hey!" Riley pulled the bowl to the side. "Leave some for the cake." She grabbed a spatula and began spreading the ganache over the largest layer. "It's not as easy to spread as I'd hoped."

"That's what he said," Brianna said quietly.

Everyone fell silent, turning amused eyes on Brianna, who hardly ever made dirty comments, and they all exploded into fits of laughter again.

"We'll never get this thing done. It's almost dinnertime." Riley continued icing the layers.

When she was done with the last layer, they washed their hands and took turns kneading the fondant with their palms. Then they rolled it flat.

"Okay, this is really tricky," Riley said, moving the largest layer of cake beside the fondant.

"I think it's ready. It's hard." Max leaned closer to the cake, inspecting it more closely.

"We like hard," Jade joked.

Riley touched the biggest layer and her heart sank. "Oh no. No, no, no."

"What? It's not supposed to get hard?" Savannah asked.

"No!" Riley glanced at the other layers, each glistening and *hard*. "The fondant needs to stick to it. This is awful. I've ruined the only surprise I have for Josh."

"Are you sure, Ri?" Jade poked the ganache. "Because I can't imagine *hard* is not good."

Riley gave her a do-not-go-there glare. "I'm sure." She tapped the hard chocolate with her spatula. "It's ruined. I totally forgot the one, two, three rule!"

"What?" Savannah arched a brow.

Riley paced. "Molly drilled it into my head, but I was so sidetracked making the ganache perfect, I forgot. Ganache, fondant, pearls. One, two, three. One layer at a time start to finish."

Charlotte breezed into the kitchen. "Mm. That looks amazing!"

"It's ruined." The confession sent the pit of Riley's stomach to her knees as Jade explained to Charlotte what had happened.

"Can't we just keep the chocolate layer and put something over it that's sticky?" Brianna suggested.

Hope filled Riley's chest. "Yes. Probably. Is there a store nearby, Charlotte?"

"There's nothing *nearby*." Charlotte eyed the cake. "But what do you need? Will strawberry jam work?"

"Yes, I think so," Riley said, silently praying it would.

"Chocolate and strawberry are delicious together," Savannah added.

"Then you're in luck." Charlotte pointed to her chest. "I am insanely addicted to Luscious Leanna's Sweet Treats jams. I have it shipped to me by the dozen. Come on. I'll show you."

As Savannah *whoop*ed and explained that her husband's brother, Kurt Remington, was married to Leanna, the woman behind Luscious Leanna's Sweet Treats, Riley thanked her lucky stars that fate had stepped into their lives once again. The wedding cake just might be perfect after all!

"OKAY, LITTLE BROTHER, get your scrawny ass up that ladder and hang those curtains." Rex gave Josh a playful shove toward the ladder and peered over the deck railing at Hope grazing in the field.

Jack looked up from where he stood beside the table and shook his head.

"Scrawny my butt. You might be able to kick my ass, but you'll never look better in a tux than I do." Having already hung the drapes on rods that would hook into the top of the canopy frame they'd built, Josh climbed the ladder. Since their wedding was taking place in the early evening, they'd hung a glass chandelier in the center. Even without the drapes, Josh could tell it would look exactly as they'd hoped, casually elegant.

"But you do build a hell of an altar," he said to Rex. "So I guess you're worth keeping around."

"Careful up there," Hugh hollered from where he was crouched beside the railings securing netting so they wouldn't spend the entire wedding chasing kids' toys that slipped through.

Donned in a pair of cargo shorts and a Brave Foundation T-shirt, Dane climbed the ladder on the opposite side of the frame to help Josh hang the drapes. Dane was neither burly like Rex nor lean like Josh. He hovered somewhere in the middle from years of diving. As a shark tagger, researcher, and the founder of the foundation, which strove to educate people about sharks with the goal of saving the species, Dane was always on the move. "Ready, bro?"

"Let's do this." Josh was excited to see the altar come to fruition. Almost as excited as he was to stand beneath it and finally become Riley's husband.

Rich coral drapes lined with sparkling gold satin and adorned with intricate lace and pearls along the edges would be layered over white sheers. After putting the drapes on the rod and then re-covering them with plastic sheathing, Josh had placed them on the table beside the rod containing the white sheers. Once hung, the vibrant drapes would be tied back with floral bouquets the girls planned to make tomorrow morning, leaving just a hint of white peeking out from beneath.

Rex and Jack reached for the drapery rod.

"Whoa," Josh said from his perch on the ladder. "We need the sheers first."

"Aw, hell. Why do you have to be so fancy?" Rex mumbled, and set the drapery rod carefully on the table.

Jack laughed. "Maybe because *fancy* is what he does for a living." He lifted the rod with the sheers, and Rex held up the other side for Dane.

Josh and Dane secured the rod and then repeated the process on the other side of the frame. The sheers, even protected in plastic, took the canopy from a rustic wooden structure to an enticing altar.

"Ready for the curtains?" Rex asked.

"Drapes," Josh corrected him.

Rex rolled his eyes as he and Jack handed the rod up to their brothers. As they worked to secure it in place, Josh thought about the wedding gift he had in store for his beautiful wife-to-be, and the decisions about where to live after the baby was born.

"Looking good." Hugh pushed to his feet and wiped his hands on his jeans.

"As long as we've got time to kill while we're doing this, I wanted to ask you guys about something." Josh secured the end of the rod onto the frame and held it in place while Dane attached his end. "What's it like to live in more than one place? I mean with your kids and your businesses. Jack, I know you and Savannah spend a lot of time in the mountains. Does it throw Adam's schedule off?"

Jack wrinkled his brow. "It throws our schedules off more than his. That kid sleeps like a log, anyplace, anytime."

"Seriously? You're lucky," Dane said, struggling to attach his side of the rod. "Hey, Rex. Hand me the hammer, will ya?" Leaning down to take the hammer, Dane said, "Finn's teething, so he has an excuse to get up a million times during the night, but even before he started getting teeth, he was a freaking night owl." He hammered at the mechanism. "I swear the only time he sleeps well is when we're awake. The minute our eyes close, he wakes up."

Rex laughed. "Guess we're lucky. Little Hal sleeps like a champ. Nothing messes with his schedule."

"It all depends on the kid and the age," Hugh added. "It's hard on Layla, and hiring private tutors when we're on the road is a hassle, not to mention getting used to different cities. Even when we get back to Virginia, there's a settling-in period. It's not a normal life, which is why I cut so far back on racing. We try to strike a balance that works for all of us. I'm glad you brought this up, though, because I have something I wanted to talk to you guys about before the wedding gets under way."

"Is Bree pregnant again?" Josh asked. He knew how much Riley was hoping their baby would have cousins close in age.

Hugh laughed. "Not yet, but not for lack of trying." He leaned against the railing, watching Josh and Dane climb down and move the ladders to the other side, only to repeat the same steps again. "We're moving back to Weston."

They all stopped what they were doing and looked at him with disbelief. Hugh and Brianna owned several houses, but they'd always kept their home base near Brianna's mother in Virginia.

Hugh pointed to Layla and Adriana in the grass with Treat, meticulously twining together flower headdresses. Both girls were smiling. Treat said something they couldn't hear and the girls broke into hysterics.

"Layla misses Adriana and the other kids. And Christian loves the activity and chaos of being around everyone. And of course he's crazy for Dylan. And they both miss Dad something awful. Layla talks about living in Weston all the time, and honestly, I'm glad to be coming back. And all that stuff we just talked about—school, schedules—that's a big part of the reason we're moving. Coming back home will cut the need for frequent trips from Virginia to Colorado." Hugh's eyes turned serious. "Nothing replaces touching base with family, and we weren't about to give that up. We're moving right after Kat and Eric's wedding this winter." Brianna's best friend, Kat Martin, was marrying one of Hugh's closest friends, a fellow race-car driver, Eric James. Eric had spent so much time with the Bradens, he was like family.

"But what about Bree's mother?" Josh asked, mentally putting another tick in favor of moving to Weston. "She'll be devastated." That thought made him wonder if Riley's parents had been sad when she'd moved to New York. They'd been so wrapped up in each other and their growing business, they hadn't spent much time worrying about her parents feeling the loss of her constant presence.

"She's moving, too. We found a property we loved on

Rosedale Lane, but we were too late making an offer. Some asshat beat me to it." Hugh hiked a thumb over his shoulder toward Treat. "Last week he hooked us up with a property that hadn't yet hit the market. Thirty acres across town. There's a guesthouse on the grounds that's perfect for Bree's mom. Dad's not getting any younger. It's time to come home."

Josh climbed down from the ladder thinking of his father keeping the kids occupied while Josh and the others prepared for the wedding. He imagined his father missed Layla and Christian just as much as they missed him. He had to admit that he not only missed his father, but he missed this, too. Being with his family had always rejuvenated him, and he knew how happy it made Riley to spend time with Jade and the other girls. And times like these, when they pulled together to help one another out, came too infrequently these days.

"Why are you asking, Josh? Are you and Ri thinking about coming home?" Hugh asked.

Dane stepped off his ladder, laughing under his breath, and put a hand on Josh's shoulder. "Getting this guy to move from the Big Apple would be like getting me to live on dry land. It ain't happening, right, Josh?"

Never say never.

The back door flew open, and Hal strode across the deck with a baby in each arm. His expression was a mixture of concern and amusement, although each determined stride told Josh that he was leaning toward the concerned side.

Rex reached for his son. "What's up? Tired of playing nanny?"

Hal wrinkled his brow. "Nanny my rear end. We have a *situation.*"

They followed Hal inside, where they found Dylan and

Christian sitting on the leather couch in the living room with marker all over their hands and shirts, their eyes as wide and scared as if they'd seen a ghost. Hal strode past the boys directly into the study.

Hugh stooped beside Christian. "What's wrong, buddy?"

Tears slid down his son's cheeks. Lifting Christian into his arms, Hugh shot a look toward their father's back, and Dylan's waterworks began. Hugh mumbled something under his breath, and Jack hoisted Dylan onto his hip.

"What's the matter, buddy?" Jack asked.

While Christian was all words all the time, Dylan tended to hold his tongue more often. He just buried his face in Jack's chest.

Rex stood at the entrance to the study, rubbing his scruff, his eyes narrow and serious. He put a hand out, thumping hard on the center of Josh's chest, stopping him from entering the study. "Don't overreact."

Josh peered around his burly brother, and his gut clenched at the sight of Riley's wedding dress, now decorated with scribbles and stick figures in a multitude of colors. Anger bubbled up inside him. His hands were fisted by his sides. He wanted to punch the wall, to holler at no one in particular, but one more look at those little boys crying big tears, and he knew he wouldn't do either.

Hugh peered around Josh. "Holy—Christian Braden, what have I told you about touching other people's things?" he said sternly, causing more waterworks to fall from his son's eyes.

Josh's heart ached for the little boy. And for Riley. They'd worked so hard on making her wedding gown perfect, and now it had been ruined at the hands of two of the cutest vandals on earth.

"We were decorating Aunt Riley's dress," Christian said through sobs. "We didn't know it was *supposed* to be boring!" He looked at Dylan, his partner in crime, his dark eyes imploring the little boy to agree, which Dylan did with several overeager nods.

Josh pulled Jack and Hugh into the room and motioned for Dane to close the doors to the study. He paced, fisting and unfisting his hands, trying to rein in his reeling emotions. As soon as the doors were closed, he said, "Lock it."

Dane did, and they all started speaking at once.

"I'm sorry," Hugh said, pacing alongside Josh.

Josh held his hands up, bringing silence to the room, save for the sounds of the little boys crying.

"The only thing that matters right now is that Riley does *not* find out about this," he said sternly.

"What are you talking about?" Rex said angrily. "You think she won't notice that her wedding gown looks like a preschool drawing table?"

"You could start a new wedding-gown trend," Dane added.

Josh glared at Dane, then ran a hand through his hair and blew out a breath, trying to think this through, but his mind was going in ten different directions. He paced the floor as he spoke. "I'll fix it. It looks like it's only the skirt that's ruined. I'll get material sent in and I'll stay up all night making a new skirt if I have to. I have to fix this."

"Son," Hal said evenly. "The wedding is *tomorrow*."

"Not to mention, if you start ordering loads of wedding dress material, you'll have the paparazzi on the next helicopter out here." Dane crossed his arms. "You have to tell her."

"No. I have to *fix* this." He shifted his gaze to his father. "Did any of the girls see this?"

Hal shook his head. "Do you think I'd still be standing here if they did? They're Riley's cavalry. They'd be all over me. I'm sorry, Josh. I let the boys out of my sight for only a few minutes while I changed the babies' diapers."

Josh looked at his sobbing nephews, and his heart broke anew. Letting out a long sigh, he said, "It's not your fault. Or theirs, really. They're kids, and you're only one person." He met his father's concerned gaze. "Despite the fact that you think you're Superman, there's no way you could have kept watch on all four of them."

Pacing, Josh reminded himself of the same things he'd just told his father, and tried not to picture Riley's face when she caught wind of this debacle. "Maybe I can call our cousin Jax in Pleasant Hill. His specialty is wedding gowns. You know he'll have it on hand. He can ship it overnight with morning delivery to—"

"Don't suggest anyone close to us, because if the paparazzi is trying to find you, then you've just given that dog a bone," Rex reminded him.

Josh cursed under his breath.

"You have to tell her," Dane said empathetically. "You're not Superman either, Josh. It was an accident. She'll be heartbroken, but she'll understand."

The truth was, Riley *would* understand, but she'd also be crushed, and that slayed Josh. "If you knew Lacy would be heartbroken, would you just say 'Oh, well,' or would you do everything within your power to fix it so she was a little less torn up?" He eyed the ruined dress, ignoring the hushed remarks coming from all directions. The boys' "decorations" were mostly along the front middle portion of the skirt. The gears of Josh's designer mind churned as he imagined cutting out the marred area and angling the hemline higher in the front. He lifted the skirt, inspecting it more closely, and realized he could probably make it work. "Think Charlotte has a working sewing machine and about a mile of"—he knew now was not the time to be picky about proper threading for a wedding gown—"white thread?"

"I'm sure her mother had one," Hal said. "She used to make all of Charlotte's clothes when Charlotte was a little girl."

"Then we need to find it. I think I can cut around the drawings and create a knee-length hem in the front. I'll wait until Riley goes to sleep and then I'll figure something out. I never thought I'd be thankful about sleeping in separate rooms."

"You can't cut up her wedding dress without asking her," Hugh said. "If I've learned one thing about women, it's that certain things are untouchable." Christian rested his cheek against Hugh's chest and wiped his tears with his fist. Hugh pressed a kiss to the top of his head.

"I know my fiancée," Josh said. "This dress meant everything to her because we designed it together. The last thing she needs is to see it ruined. At least this way, she may be upset, but she'll have a beautiful white gown that she can get married in."

"I'm sorry, Uncle Josh," Christian said, tears still streaming down his cheeks.

"My mommy can wash it in the washing machine," Dylan suggested. "That's what she does at home."

Despite the ache growing inside his chest for Riley, Josh smiled. "I wish that would fix it, little man."

Christian clung to his father's shirt, and Dylan burrowed against Jack's chest. Josh didn't blame him, because just thinking about Riley catching wind of what happened to her dress made him want to hide someplace safe, too.

"I know you were trying to help Riley make her dress prettier," he said to the boys. "And that's a really thoughtful thing to do. You're both very creative, which is a good thing."

"Thank you," they mumbled.

"But as fun as it is to help Aunt Riley look beautiful for her wedding, you should always ask before making other people's things look better, okay?"

The boys nodded again. The look Hugh gave him—one of gratitude and approval—brought another wave of emotions to Josh.

Focusing on the kids, he said, "Here's the deal. Aunt Riley *likes* her dress a little *boring*."

Christian wrinkled his nose in obvious disagreement.

Josh was completely taken with the little rascals, despite how bad the situation was. "I have a plan that will help make this situation better, but you'll both need to help me make it right for Aunt Riley. Can you do that?"

Nodding emphatically, their tears stopped.

"You can't tell anyone about this," Dane said.

Josh gave his brother a wry smile. "I don't know much about parenting, but I'm pretty sure we shouldn't teach them to keep secrets from adults."

"Man, you sound like Bree," Hugh said.

Josh cocked his head toward his father, and Hal winked. Hal had always made Josh take responsibility for his actions. Usually that meant Josh had to apologize to someone or clean out the horse stalls. Though it didn't happen often, when it did, it made an impact. But there would be no apologizing to Riley before he had a chance to fix her dress. The best he could hope for was keeping the boys as far away from the girls as possible so they didn't accidentally let it slip.

"Okay, here's the deal, boys. I need you to stick close by Grandpa Hal this evening…"

Chapter Four

THE LATE AFTERNOON took a busy turn. Riley and the girls were sidetracked from the cake by hungry children, cranky babies, and men who needed nourishment. It was nearly eight thirty, and Riley and Josh were finishing the dishes while the girls and their husbands put their children to bed. Riley loved that the husbands and wives handled bedtime together. She imagined her and Josh doing the same once their baby was born. Hal was outside with Hope, and Riley's parents were due to arrive any minute. She was happy to have a moment alone with Josh.

"How did the cake turn out?" Josh asked as he dried a bowl.

She and Jade had wrapped the wedding cake layers and put them out of sight before dinner. They'd finish frosting it after the children were settled and the men had reconvened some-place *other* than the kitchen.

"We had to make a minor adjustment to the recipe, but it's going to be delicious."

Josh set down the towel he was using to dry the dishes and moved behind her. He gathered her hair over one shoulder and brushed his lips over her cheek, wrapping his strong arms around her waist. She closed her eyes, relaxing into his embrace.

They'd been moving at breakneck speed since last night, when they'd left the resort, and all she wanted to do was curl up in his arms and be loved by him.

"I've missed you," she whispered as he kissed his way down her neck. With her eyes still closed, she felt for the faucet and turned it off, enjoying every blessed second of the alone time with her soon-to-be husband.

Josh turned her in his arms, and when she reached for the towel to dry her hands, he took her hands in his and guided them around his waist.

She scrunched her nose. "I'm wet."

"That's what I like to hear," he whispered seductively.

She giggled, but he was all hands and lips, groping her ass as he sank his teeth into her neck and sucked so hard heat seared between her legs, turning that short-lived giggle into a needy moan. She craned her neck to the side, giving him better access to continue his tantalizing assault, but he grasped the back of her skull, angling her mouth beneath his, and took her in a kiss so intense she lost all sense of place and time. Reveling in the feel of Josh's hands holding, caressing, *taking*, and his eager mouth, she went up on her toes in an effort to get more of him. Then his hands were on her hips, lifting her onto the counter without breaking their connection. Riley had always been amazed at the way he lifted her so easily. She was not a petite girl. She had real womanly curves, which Josh seemed to have an insatiable appetite for. Thank goodness, because she was only going to get curvier with her pregnancy.

"God, I love you," he said between frantic kisses. He tugged the neckline of her shirt down and kissed the flesh he bared, filling his other hand with her breast.

Her nipples pebbled, burning with the need to be in his

mouth. Tugging her forward, he pressed his arousal to her center, and she was incapable of holding back another moan.

"Josh," she said breathlessly. "Kiss me."

And he did.

Hard. So exquisitely perfectly, she yanked up on his shirt, needing to feel his skin beneath her hands. He grabbed her legs and wrapped them around his hips, lifting her off the counter as she explored his muscular back.

"Oh, goodness!"

Riley's eyes flew open at the sound of her mother's voice. "Mom!" She'd been so lost in Josh, she'd forgotten that anyone could walk in. She had Josh's shirt up around his shoulders, her legs around his waist. She tried to shimmy out of Josh's arms, but he moved carefully, slowing her down, and she knew he was being careful because of the baby. She loved him for it, but with her mother turning bright red and her father sauntering into the kitchen behind her, she *really* needed to put some space between them. Her parents didn't need to see her practically tearing off Josh's clothes.

"I'm sorry," her mother said with a knowing grin that unsettled Riley even more. "We knocked, but no one answered."

"We were...um...just..." *Nearly going at it right here in the kitchen!* Riley frantically smoothed her top and tried to blink away the lust fog from her brain. The fact that Josh was rearranging his shirt to hide his hard-on wasn't making it any easier.

Josh kissed her cheek, smiling in that easy way that usually made her sigh—but this time it just felt unfair. How did he remain calm every single time something went awry?

"We were making out," he said without apology. "But we'll all pretend we weren't."

Her mother laughed. "Why on earth would we pretend that? Love is a beautiful thing." Her mother stepped forward and hugged Josh, while Riley tried to get over feeling like a naughty teenager caught behind the bleachers.

"Come over here, sunshine." Her father pulled her into a warm embrace. He was tall and slim, so different from Josh's father, quieter, too. He held her for a long moment, then kissed the top of her head and greeted Josh while her mother hugged the daylights out of her.

"I'm sorry we're so late," her mother said. "One thing after another went wrong when we were trying to get out of the house. Then we got halfway here and realized we had forgotten our bags. So we had to drive back home and get them. I swear my brain has gone on vacation."

"I'm sorry it was such a hassle, but I'm glad you're here," Riley said. "You can help me finish making the cake."

"I have to admit," her father said. "I was a little worried that because of your social status in the city, you'd feel pressure to give the public what they so obviously want. I'm glad you went with an intimate gathering."

"It was an easy decision for us, although it wasn't easy avoiding the cameras." Josh put his arm around Riley and kissed her temple. "But it was worth the sneaking around to get the wedding we both wanted."

"Have you heard from Jake or the others since you left the Bahamas?" her mother asked.

"Yes. As a matter of fact, Jake called earlier and said he let it leak to the press that Riley and I came down with food poisoning," Josh said, surprising Riley. "We are supposedly holed up in the honeymoon suite at the resort right this very second."

She'd like to be holed up with Josh somewhere despite how happy she was to see them.

"It's a shame your extended family couldn't be together," her mother said. "You could have had a triple wedding."

"It would have been nice to have everyone together, and we talked about it, but we really didn't want the chaos that came along with it," Riley explained. "Just getting out of the Bahamas was crazy enough. I still feel guilty that everyone had to play along with our ruse."

Josh pulled her tight against his side. "They didn't mind. And besides, you shouldn't feel too bad. Jake and Ross *are* marrying their fiancées in a double ceremony tomorrow at the resort."

"I know, but still." When they'd put the ruse together, Josh's cousins Jake and Ross had decided it was silly to waste a gorgeous wedding venue. They and their fiancées didn't seem to mind a little publicity.

Jade, Savannah, and Lacy came into the kitchen with Max and Brianna on their heels.

"You made it!" Jade hugged Riley's mother, which started a flurry of eager greetings.

Josh kissed Riley and whispered, "I think I'll save your dad from the estrogen overload and take him out back with the guys." He pulled her into his arms and kissed her.

Riley wound her arms around his neck. "This is our last night as a unmarried couple. I had fun doing the dishes with you."

"Baby, I'd do so much more with you if we had privacy. Maybe we should ditch these guys and find a quiet coatroom." A spark of heat flared in his eyes.

"We do have an affinity for coatrooms." She and Josh had

snuck into a coatroom at Christos to fool around the night Josh proposed.

His hands slid to her butt and he squeezed. "I have an affinity for you, babe. In the coatroom, the boardroom, the bedroom, the dining room…" He kissed her again, long and lovingly, and it was so good to be in his arms, having her wits about her this time, she didn't mind that her parents were in the room. She could control herself.

For a little while, anyway.

IT WAS AFTER eleven, and the men had turned in already in preparation for the early-rising babies. There was no way the girls would be up early, since they were all spending the night together in the biggest suite at the resort. Riley told them they didn't have to sleep in the same room with her, but they insisted. Not only that, they moved mattresses to the floor with fluffy pillows and blankets, like a giant sleepover. Even her mother said she was going to stay with them, for most of the night, anyway. Riley couldn't wait. As ridiculous as it sounded, she was excited to have this time alone with the girls. They'd broken out the wine and the box of brownies Elisabeth had given Riley, and everyone was sipping the good stuff and chowing down. Except Riley. She couldn't drink because of her pregnancy, and after the ganache fiasco, she was too nervous about preparing the cake to even *think* about eating.

They'd finally stopped chatting long enough to frost the cakes with the jam Charlotte had given them. They'd used several jars, and Riley was pleased with the addition to the recipe. She kneaded the fondant until it was the perfect consistency, just as Molly had taught her to do, and now they were taking turns rolling four portions of fondant to frost each layer of the cake.

"What do you think Hal did to keep his sons from turning into self-centered jerks?" Max stood in the open doorway, looking out over the deck. "Because whatever it is, I want to do it with Dylan. I hate jerky guys."

Jade laughed and grabbed another brownie. "You mean because of their good looks, or as I like to call it, the 'Braden curse'? Haven't you learned that Hal's influence is bigger than any curse could ever be?"

"Hey, way to leave me out. I'm a Braden, too," Savannah complained, stuffing another piece of brownie in her mouth.

"And gorgeous as the day is long," Riley said.

"Aw, thanks almost-sis-in-law." Savannah gave her a sticky kiss on her cheek. "Dad would never have put up with us being jerks, but my brothers had their moments. While I was a perfect angel," she said with an air of sarcasm.

"Looks don't make the jerk. Jerks make the jerk." Lacy laughed at her own joke. "Sometimes I try to imagine Dane bald."

Max laughed, and a piece of brownie shot out of her mouth, causing an uproar of hysterical laughter.

"Shh," Riley said. "Everyone's sleeping."

"It wouldn't matter if Jack were bald. I'd still be all over him." Savannah opened a cabinet and pulled out a bag of chips. As she dumped them into a bowl, Brianna grabbed two and put them on either side of her brownie. Savannah arched a brow.

"What?" Brianna took a bite of the chip-brownie sandwich. With a mouthful, she said, "Sweet and salty is the bomb."

At that, Savannah and Max each piled chips on their brownies and stuffed them into their mouths, emitting a loud, "Mm."

"I'd like to add 'Banks curse' to that, please," Riley's mother said. "My hubby might not be rugged, but he's strong in all the ways that matter, and I adore him."

Riley looked up from the fondant she was working with, feeling thankful for the love in her mother's voice. There was a time when she thought her parents had a less-than-passionate marriage. Her mother had explained that in any marriage desires waxed and waned, but that didn't mean it wasn't a good marriage that was full of love and commitment. When those amorous feelings waned, she and Riley's father worked harder to rekindle the passion. Riley couldn't imagine ever not getting all revved up by merely catching sight of her smoking-hot fiancé, but if that time ever came, she hoped they could take a page from her mother's marriage book and rekindle the spark rather than let it go out.

"He's definitely on the list, Mrs. B," Jade said, handing the roller to Lacy so she could take her turn rolling the fondant. "I need to get another brownie and try it with chips. Want one?"

"Of course. Everyone knows you can't have just one." Lacy began rolling the fondant.

"Mrs. B," Jade said as she made two chip-brownie sandwiches. "Your man is as cursed as the rest of them, and I adore him, too. Even if he was a little strict with my girl Riley when she was younger."

"Let's not relive my teen years," Riley pleaded. "Besides, it's time to finish the cake, and I'm sure I need all hands on deck for this one."

"You mean you don't want to remember how you pined for Josh every minute of the day?" Jade asked.

The girls and her mother gathered around the table, licking

their fingers and nibbling on chips.

Riley figured she must be really on edge, because all she could hear was one smacking noise after another. "I didn't pine."

Her mother's brows lifted over amused eyes.

Riley sighed. "Whatever. Maybe there was a little pining going on, but I don't think it was *that* obvious."

Savannah giggled.

"Was it that obvious?" Lacy stuffed her brownie into her mouth, making her cheeks puffy.

"You look like a chipmunk hoarding nuts," Max pointed out.

"I bet Dane has big nuts," Brianna said with a laugh, then smacked her hand over her mouth like she couldn't believe she'd said that.

"Bree! My mother is in the room!" Riley reminded her.

"Sorry," Bree mumbled from behind her hand, but there was no hiding the laughter coming from her and from Max.

"Oh, honey," her mother said, picking up a crumb from the now empty brownie box and licking it off her fingers. "I like *nuts* just as much as any other woman does."

Riley felt her cheeks burn. "Mom. That is *not* something I need to know about you."

"Thinking about my parents doing dirty stuff isn't a great visual," Jade said, and quickly added, "Not that you aren't hot, Mrs. B. It's just—"

"Trust me." Her mother took a gulp of her wine. "When you get to be my age, it's not about how hard the body is. It's about if the body has the ability to get hard."

"Mom!" Mortified, Riley took her mother's wineglass and set it on the counter. "I think you've had enough. Your eyes are glassy. How much have you had to drink?"

Her mother grabbed the glass and waved Riley off. "Since when did you become so prudish, Riley Roo? It's your pre-wedding night. *Live* a little."

"Ohmygod." Riley rolled her eyes.

"Riley's not a prude, Mrs. B," Max said. "She's as naughty as the rest of them."

"Including you," Brianna said around a mouthful of chips.

Riley ran her eyes around the table and realized they were *all* eating chips. Over the fondant. "Oh my God. No, no, no. Please don't get crumbs in the fondant." She walked around the table gently moving each of them back a few steps. "I'm having visions of salty, chip-tasting fondant on my wedding cake. What is up with you guys? It's like you haven't eaten in a month. Why don't you bring out the leftovers from dinner while you're at it?"

Savannah's eyes widened. "Great idea!" She and Lacy head-ed for the refrigerator. "Did you know there are haunted rooms here?"

"No way." Lacy carried a plate of chicken to the counter, and Riley's mother began cutting it up.

"Way," Savannah said. She set a bowl of potato salad beside the chicken. "Charlotte told me that the suite we're staying in is one of them."

"We totally have to exorcise them," Lacy said. "I can do that. I read about it."

"I'm reading this book about auras," Max said as she handed forks to each of the girls. "Kaylie Crew lent it to me, and I swear, Mrs. B, yours is violet, which fits you perfectly because you're very wise." Max had met Treat at her boss Chaz's wedding. Kaylie was Chaz's wife.

Her mom laughed. "I don't think I'm very wise."

"Yes, you are, Mom. *You're* reading about auras, Max?" Riley asked. "That doesn't seem like your thing." While the girls gobbled down food like there was no tomorrow, Riley began applying the fondant.

Max spread her hands out in front of her as if she were presenting something and said, "I'm expanding my horizons."

"What's my aura?" Lacy patted her wild blond curls and wiggled her shoulders. "Blue? Because I love blue. Or maybe red. That means passionate, doesn't it? That's me." She giggled and popped a piece of chicken into her mouth. "I'm all about passion."

"Orange," Max said, waving her hands like she was mimicking washing windows. "Big and orange."

"I need air." Savannah grabbed Brianna's hand. "Walk with me."

Brianna grabbed a handful of chips as Savannah dragged her out the door.

"Be careful!" Riley called after them.

"I am *not* orange. I look awful in orange." Lacy paced. "Your aura detector is broken."

"Nope. Orange," Max said.

"Like Cheetos?" Jade asked. "Lacy, Cheetos are to die for. Maybe that's not so bad."

"We have to fix it!" Lacy nodded, her eyes wide and glassy. "Fix my aura, please. And why is it *big*? Is big good or bad?"

"Orange won't do," Riley's mother said. "Big is okay…I think."

"Fix me, please!" Lacy grabbed Max's hand. "You have to fix it. I can't be orange. Dane hates orange."

As if they were speaking in some strange tongue Riley didn't understand, the rest of them—including her mother—hurried toward the stairs with promises of new auras. And with the bowl of chips. Leaving Riley to wonder why the hell everyone had lost their minds. That must have been some potent wine they were drinking. Longing for a sip of the nectar, she glanced at her mother's glass, and her hand drifted to her belly.

It's worth giving up a few things for you, little one.

Remembering how quickly fondant set, she picked up her pace, applying it on top of the jam as the girls disappeared up the stairs. Riley was thankful for a little quiet so she could concentrate on making each layer perfect. She smoothed and edged and rubbed out air bubbles, then carefully stacked the layers and smoothed each one again. Once that was done, she began applying the decorative pearls around the base of the bottom two layers. She worked tirelessly, meticulously pressing each pearl into the fondant, creating waves of the tiny white and silver beads. Finally, she spelled out "R & J" on opposite sides of the second layer. When that was done, she let out a long breath, feeling as though she'd just run a marathon. How could concentrating be so exhausting?

Stepping back from the table, she admired her work. The layers weren't entirely even, and there was a tiny pinch in the fondant that she didn't want to wrestle with for fear of the cake toppling over. Even still, her gift to Josh was done, and it looked pretty damn good. All that was left was placing the small red, pink, and white rose bouquet she'd had Jade bring with her on the top of the cake, and a few sweetheart roses on the layers to really bring it to life.

In the quiet of the kitchen, with the cool mountain air streaming in through the open door, she washed her hands and caught a peek of the canopied altar Josh and the others had built. It was exactly as they'd pictured it, equally elegant and casual, and bold without being overbearing. She loved knowing it was built at the hands of Josh's family.

Built with love. Just like the cake.

Returning her attention to the cake, she splayed her hand over her belly, thinking about how much their lives were about to change. When the inevitable *what ifs* came, she refused to give them any credence. This was a sight she would remember forever, and she wasn't going to allow anything to ruin it.

Wanting to capture the moment, she reached into her pocket for her phone to take pictures of the cake and the canopy and saw that she'd missed two calls and several text messages from Elisabeth. She'd silenced her phone when Finn had fallen asleep in Lacy's arms after dinner, and she must have forgotten to turn it back on.

She quickly scrolled through the text bubbles.

Don't eat the brownies! I accidentally gave you the medicinal brownies I made for Mrs. Phillips!

Are you there? Answer your phone!

They're marijuana brownies!

Holy. Shit.

Riley didn't bother reading the rest of the messages. Her eyes snapped to the empty brownie box. No wonder they were eating everything in sight. They were all high. They had the munchies! Her mind darted in a hundred directions at once, and she realized Savannah and Brianna hadn't come back inside. Her heart raced as she ran outside and scanned the grounds. It was too dark to see very far. She hurried down the steps and called out in a hushed whisper so as not to wake anyone up.

"Bree? Savannah?" She hurried across the backyard, racing the full length of the massive resort, scanning the property and calling for them. "Savannah? Bree?"

Panic swelled in her chest with every passing second. She caught sight of movement by the lake and sprinted toward it. "Savannah? Bree?"

Hope *neigh*ed, and Riley followed the noise. The chestnut horse came into view at the water's edge. Her big head bobbed up and down toward the water. Riley squinted into the darkness as she ran, praying they hadn't drowned.

"Savannah? Brianna?" she shouted, not caring who she woke up.

Silence.

"Savannah! Brianna!"

Giggles came from somewhere ahead of her in the darkness, and the water rippled against the shore. Relieved, and slightly pissed over their silence, she tried her hardest to find a modicum of control, but her voice burst from her lungs.

"Goddamn it! Where are you?"

She stepped forward, nearly tripping on a pile of clothes. Splashing sounded somewhere in front of her. Putting two and two together, she didn't know whether to laugh or strangle them.

"Get out of there. You shouldn't be skinny-dipping!"

"Come in, Ri!" Savannah yelled. "Nothing feels as good as this."

"Except sex!" Brianna yelled. Their laughter filled the air.

Riley grabbed their clothes, realizing how out of character everything Brianna had said tonight had been, and...*Holy hell. Mom!*

"You guys, get out here now. You're totally stoned! The brownies had pot in them!" She had to find her mother. Hopefully she and the others were sleeping it off somewhere.

More giggling ensued.

"This isn't funny. You shouldn't be swimming when you're high. Get out of there!" Her every nerve was on fire, and she was holding on to her last shred of control. When they laughed again, she nearly blew her top. "I'll come in there and drag you out before I let you drown the night before my wedding!"

More giggling, splashing, and then their smiling faces appeared in a streak of moonlight.

"Fine," Brianna grumbled. She and Savannah strode out of the water naked, oblivious to the chilly night air. "What were you yelling about the brownies?"

"Did you find more? I want more brownies," Savannah said with a glimmer of hope in her eyes.

"No more brownies." She shoved their clothes into their hands. "We have to find the others. There was pot in the brownies, and you guys are completely stoned."

"*Pfft.*" Savannah strutted ahead of her, buck-naked, clutching her clothes to her chest. "We are not."

"Nope," Brianna agreed. She stumbled and grabbed Riley's shirt, pulling them both down to the ground. Brianna rolled in the grass, laughing hysterically, while Riley pushed to her feet with a protective hand over her belly, glad she'd landed on her butt.

Savannah stared absently up at the moon. She lifted her hand and began opening and closing her fingers. "I can't grab it."

"Are you fucking kidding me? This is my pre-wedding night? Babysitting two stoned women?"

Brianna stopped laughing, then started again, still lying on the ground. Her hands and legs were stretched out as far as they could go. "Vannah! Come here!"

Savannah turned, and Riley grabbed her arm. "Oh, no, you don't. No more stargazing for you two." She reached down and pulled Brianna up by her arm. "We have to go find the others. And get you towels, clothes, and beds."

"I'm not tired," Brianna complained. "I'm hungry."

Several long, frustrating minutes later Riley finally managed to get them to comply, and they headed up to the kitchen. "Stand on the deck and I'll be right back with towels."

She ran upstairs and grabbed two towels, then ran back downstairs and gave them to the girls. "I have to find—"

Thump. Thump. Thump.

She lifted her eyes toward the noise coming from upstairs, wondering what the hell *that* was. "Dry off and go upstairs to our suite, okay? I have to check on that noise."

Hurrying upstairs, Riley followed the sounds. She had no idea how the men and children could sleep through the banging. Following the sounds down the wide hallway to the suite where they were staying, she pushed the heavy double doors open and nearly lost her lunch. Her mother stood by an enormous hole in the wall, holding a lamp like a baseball bat. The lampshade and lightbulb lay forgotten a few feet away. Max swung a shoe at the broken drywall, chipping off another piece. And Lacy, whose face was smeared with something that looked like lipstick, was...*chanting*.

Holy mother of all things crazy, what the flip was going on now?

Her mother swung the lamp.

"Stop!" Riley commanded, and three sets of eyes turned to her. She grabbed the lamp from her mother's hands. "Stop. Don't move. Don't swing, hit, or chant." She took the shoe from Max's hands, which were covered in red, like Lacy's face.

"Why would you do this?"

Max wiped her face, smearing red across her nose and cheeks. "We're excavating the ghosts."

Lacy nodded, wide-eyed.

"Exorcising, sweetie," her mother said, stumbling backward.

"Oh God. This is Charlotte's *house*." She felt sick to her stomach. "You've put a *hole* in her *house*."

Her mother stumbled to the bed and flopped down. "We did her a favor. Freeing the ghosts."

Lacy grabbed Riley's arm. "We had to do it, or who knows what the ghosts would do. They could have been evil, or like…like…that movie *The Entity*. Yeah. They could have been like that." She looked around the room with a serious expression. "Where's Savannah? I have to tell her it's safe now." She headed for the door, and Riley grabbed her.

"Oh no, you don't. You need to go into the bathroom and wash off whatever that is on your face."

Lacy palmed her face and shook her head, smearing the red onto her neck. "I'm *not* taking off my aura! Max worked hard to fix me, and Dane will love my red aura. It's passionate!"

Max ran to her side. "You're right, you're not. No, Riley. She *needs* to be red."

"Passionate," her mother said from where she was now lying on the bed on her back, her legs hanging halfway off the edge.

How the hell did she get from her moment of glory downstairs to *this*? She was being punked. Or in a nightmare. She pinched herself, and it hurt like hell. *Nope. Not a nightmare.*

"Jaaaack." Savannah's voice filtered up the hall.

"Shit. Stay here," Riley commanded, and ran out of the suite, only to find Savannah disappearing, *naked*, into Riley's parents' bedroom.

Thump, thump sounded behind her.

Riley stopped cold in the hallway, midway between the bedroom where her father was about to be woken up by a naked woman and the suite where the wall was being demolished. In the space of a few panicked seconds, she figured her father waking up to a naked woman in his bed was worse than the wall getting even more damaged. She ran toward her parents' bedroom, tossing up another prayer that the kids wouldn't wake up, and flew into the room. Good fucking Lord, her night had just gone from bizarre to outrageous. Savannah was fast asleep beside her father, her long arm draped across his chest, and somehow, by the grace of God and all things magical, her father was still sleeping.

She peeled Savannah off of her father as quietly and carefully as she could, while cringing with each *thump* coming from down the hall.

"Jack," Savannah complained.

"Shh, honey, that's not Jack," she whispered. *And I don't think Jack would appreciate this one bit.* She grabbed a throw blanket from a chair and draped it around Savannah. Once outside her father's room, she closed the door and breathed a little easier, although the thunderous noises coming from down the hall ratcheted up her panic. She draped one arm around Savannah's waist and the other beneath her arm and guided her toward the suite.

"Jack," Savannah said again.

"I'll get Jack." Once inside the suite, she closed the doors and set Savannah on the edge of the bed. "Stay," she commanded, and turned to her mother, who was standing with her knees slightly bent, lamp in hands, choked up like a pro ball player. Max and Lacy were gone, but Riley heard voices coming from the bathroom.

"Mom! Stop!" Riley yelled.

Her mother stopped midswing and lowered the lamp, her eyes suddenly filling with recognition. "Riley Roo. Do you think the vortex is big enough now?" She dropped the lamp and set her hands on her hips, eyeing the hole in the wall with pride. Wiping her brow, she let out a loud sigh. "Perfect. Now those spirits can fly free."

Resigning herself to a night of crazy, Riley nodded in agreement. "Yup. You sure did a good job. Now, let's just lie down, okay, Mom? I have to find Max and Lacy." She guided her mother back to the bed, where she flopped down on her back beside Savannah. The two of them gazed up at the ceiling. Short burst of giggles escaped their lips. She draped a blanket over Savannah's naked body and hoped she and her mom would fall asleep.

Savannah's hand snuck out from beneath the cover, and she grabbed Riley's mother's hand. "Do you think she's here? Looking down on us? If she's here, I don't want her to go out the vortex."

Riley's throat swelled. A strange feeling came over her, realizing for maybe the first time ever the connection between her mother and Savannah's mother. She knew her. She wasn't her best friend, like Jade's mother had been, but she *knew* her. The realization that her mother knew the woman Josh and his siblings never had a chance to brought tears to her eyes and made her want to share her mother with them more than she already had. It also made her appreciate the time she had with her mother even more. She had the strange and sudden urge to tell her about the baby, and she realized she wanted the pieces of her mother Josh and Savannah could never have with their own.

That brought a wave of guilt so strong she reached for the dresser to stabilize herself.

"Did you hear that?" Lacy's voice trailed out of the bathroom, dragging Riley from her thoughts, right back into crazyland.

Pushing her emotions down deep, she headed for the bathroom, where she found Max and Lacy drawing on the walls with lipstick. She closed her eyes for a beat, reminding herself this was the marijuana and alcohol taking over. Her friends had not suddenly lost their minds. When she opened them, they were using that lipstick to paint each other's toenails.

Perfect.

At least there were no lamps involved.

Riley stepped quietly from the bathroom and closed the door, hoping to keep them in one place long enough for them to stay out of trouble while she went in search of Brianna.

On the way to the stairs she heard Jade's voice. *Oh crap!* She'd forgotten all about Jade. She followed the sound of her friend's voice down to...Josh's bedroom? Pushing the door open, she found Jade on the bed, where she was lying beside Brianna, who was sprawled out on her stomach, still naked, with only a towel covering her butt.

Riley couldn't even begin to take apart this situation. "Where's Josh?"

Jade giggled and pointed to Brianna.

Riley crossed her arms and glared at her. "Not Brianna. *Josh.* My future husband. That is if I don't slaughter everyone tonight."

Jade shrugged and settled in beside Brianna, with one arm draped protectively over her back.

Closing the door behind her, Riley stepped from the room

and blew out a breath. Where the hell was Josh? She knocked on Rex's door, and when he didn't answer, she knocked louder. The man must sleep like the dead. She pushed the door open and went to the side of the bed, where Rex lay in nothing but a pair of tight briefs, one arm stretched over his eyes. *Holy fucking hell.* She forced her eyes to remain *above* his waist. She hadn't thought about how awkward this would be. The man was built like the Incredible Hulk. All he needed was green paint.

"Rex," she whispered.

He didn't move.

"Rex!" she said louder, nudging his arm.

His eyes blinked open, and he bolted upright. "What's wrong? Are Jade and my boy okay?"

"Little Hal's sleeping. And if you call 'high as a kite and sleeping with Brianna, who's buck naked, okay,' then yeah. I'd say Jade's just dandy."

In three seconds flat he pulled on his jeans and was out the bedroom door. "High? Jade doesn't smoke or do drugs. She doesn't even drink much anymore."

Riley ran after him, holding his massive arm to stop him from barging into any bedrooms. "Hold on. Bree's naked. I should have gotten Hugh first, but I didn't think of it."

"Riley, you have three seconds to tell me why you said my wife is high or I'm going in anyway."

"She ate brownies laced with marijuana. They all did." She crossed her arms to protect herself from the death stare he was giving her. "It's not my fault! Elisabeth gave them to me by accident. Just...Stay here." Not knowing what stage of undress Hugh slept in, she quickly changed her mind. "Wait. I'll stay here. You get Hugh. I've seen enough Braden skivvies for one night. Except my man's. God, I need him right now."

Rex's biceps flexed, a sure sign of his fighting the urge to barge into the bedroom and claim his wife.

"I'll go in with her," she promised. "Please get your brothers and Jack. *Please?*"

He reluctantly strode away, barreling into Hugh's room without even knocking. She couldn't make out what they were saying, but heard their low baritone voices. Riley peeked into the room where Jade and Brianna were sleeping, and found them in the same position she'd left them.

Seconds later Hugh came out of the bedroom carrying a bathrobe. Rex was on his heels, and without a word, they disappeared into Treat and Jack's rooms. In what felt like only ten more seconds, all of Josh's brothers and Jack were looming over her, peppering her with questions. She held up her hands to silence them.

"Elisabeth sent brownies. They were laced with pot. We didn't know, and they ate them. *And half the kitchen.* Hugh, you better go in first and get Brianna dressed. Rex, when he comes out, you go in." She looked at the others and motioned for them to follow her. "It's not pretty in there," she said outside the door to the suite.

Treat reached for the door.

"Wait," Riley said. "Jack, you go first, because Savannah was also naked."

Jack made a growling noise that sent goose bumps racing up Riley's arm.

"It's not my fault," she reiterated.

Jack disappeared into the room for what felt like forever but in reality was only a minute or two. He appeared again cradling Savannah in his arms with the blanket tucked around her. "It's a mess in there," he said to Treat.

With a glance at Hugh and Dane, Treat pushed past Jack and led them inside. Riley's mother was fast asleep on the bed.

"Where is she?" Treat demanded.

Riley pointed to the bathroom door. "With Lacy."

"Oh, sweetness," Treat whispered with so much emotion it made Riley ache.

"Baby," Dane said, following his brother toward the bathroom.

"Thanks, Riley," Jack said. "You going to be okay?"

Riley nodded, but in truth, she was about a hundred different types of *not* okay. She was tired and still in shock from the night from hell. What if she'd eaten the brownies? What if the kids had gotten into them? And poor Charlotte's house was ruined. She was so far from okay, she couldn't even spell it.

Jack and Treat both promised to help her clean up in the morning as they carried their wives out of the bedroom. Dane was the last to leave the room, having taken the time to wash the lipstick off of Lacy's face.

"Ri," he said with Lacy in his arms. "Don't sweat any of this. Josh already called our cousin Beau and made arrangements for him to spend a few weeks shoring up things around here for Char. We'll add the wall and the bathroom to the list. We've got this, okay?"

She nodded, more grateful for her soon-to-be husband's and his brother's thoughtfulness than they could possibly know.

"Dane," Lacy said sleepily. "My aura is red, right?"

He kissed her forehead. "Yes, babe."

"Do you know where Josh is?" Riley asked. "He wasn't in his room."

A pained look crossed Dane's face. Lacy stirred in his arms, and he whispered, "He's in the east wing, but you didn't hear it from me."

With that mysterious answer swirling around in her mind, and the mayhem calmed, she decided not to wake her mother, and headed down the back staircase toward the east wing.

Chapter Five

TWO HOURS. THAT'S how long Josh had been holed up alone in a suite with Riley's wedding gown and an ancient sewing machine. Most of that time was spent sketching and perfecting the redesign of Riley's wedding dress, and the rest was spent pacing, trying to talk himself into making that first cut into her gorgeous gown. Scissors in hand, he approached the long wooden table where the dress was spread out like a sacrificial lamb waiting for slaughter. He raised the scissors, and the pang in his gut he'd been struggling against returned. He couldn't take scissors to the dress they'd spent months designing. He ran his fingers over the colorful stick figures along the center of the skirt and smiled. What if it were their child who had "decorated" the dress? Would he want to cast their creations away simply because the child had chosen the wrong canvas?

The answer came easily. *No way.*

Raking a hand through his thick hair, Josh knew what he had to do. He rubbed the back of his neck, thinking about how he should break the news to Riley. But no matter how he tried to cushion it, she would be devastated, because beneath her strong exterior was a sweet, sensitive heart that had been dead set on wearing this sparkling-white wedding gown when they exchanged their vows.

He set the scissors down beside the dress, rested his hands on the table, and sighed, allowing his shoulders to relax and his head to fall forward. He closed his eyes, grasping once again for the right words to explain the situation, and the guts to go find Riley.

"Josh?"

Josh's eyes sprang open at the sound of Riley's shaky voice. He turned, immediately struck by her frazzled state. Her eyes were wide and troubled and her hair was tousled, framing her tight expression. Her gaze dropped to the dress spread out on the table, and confusion filled her eyes.

"Babe." He reached for her, but she walked past his extended hand as if in a daze, her eyes scanning the length of the gown, hovering over the children's drawings. "I can explain."

Her jaw gaped, and she shifted her eyes to him, closed her mouth tightly, and looked at the dress again.

"Baby, the kids were only alone for a few minutes. They were trying to decorate it, to make the dress less plain." Why did this sound at least a little better in his head?

"Wh-what...?" Tears brimmed in her eyes as she gathered the dress in her arms and hugged it to her chest. Layers of tulle bunched beneath her trembling hands.

"My father was watching them, and he turned away to change the babies' diapers." He felt like he was tattling. He didn't even want to say the boys' names. "I'm sorry. I wish I could have stopped it."

She didn't say a word, which was harder to take than if she blew her top. Blinking away tears, she reached for his drawings, looking them over for a long moment. The air in the room seemed to disappear. Or maybe that was just his lungs constricting.

He touched her chin, bringing her eyes to his. "I'll fix it right now if you want me to. I've got everything I need. I was just coming to discuss it with you."

"When did this happen?" she asked just above a whisper.

Josh's chest tightened even more. "This afternoon."

"And you thought you could redesign and fix the dress *tonight*, after sleeping only a few hours last night?" She lifted the dress between them. "With all these layers?"

A disbelieving laugh bubbled up from her lungs, but it was the tear sliding down her cheek that tore open Josh's heart. He brushed it away with his fingertips and nodded. "I've got Charlotte's mother's sewing machine and what I hope is enough white thread, but that's a little iffy. I figured even if we had to use cream, it was better than—"

She pressed her lips to his, and he gathered her close, confused and thankful at once. Her dress crumpled between them, and tears slipped into their lips, turning their kiss as salty as it was sweet.

"I love that you would do that for me," she said through her tears.

"I couldn't do it. I couldn't cut the dress. Not without your approval. Every time I tried, something stopped me. I remembered the night we were designing the bodice and how when I suggested rose appliqués, your eyes lit up like I'd just promised you the world. And all those mornings I woke up and found you poring over our drawings, tweaking and rethinking, with so much energy it was like you'd already had three cups of coffee."

He touched his forehead to hers and said, "I'm so sorry, Riley. I'm sorry we had to sneak away from the Bahamas, and I'm sorry about your dress, and, God, you're shaking." He searched her eyes, and there were too many emotions looking back at him to pick them apart. "We can do this all over again. Skip the wedding and do it next weekend, after we fix your dress—"

"No," she said, shaking her head emphatically. She spread the dress over the table and turned back toward Josh, fisting her hands in his shirt. "I don't want to wait to get married. We've already waited forever." She looked forlornly at the dress again. "We worked so hard on the dress, and this…" She ran her hand over the children's drawings, breathing harder once again. "Maybe we just need to spin it positive. Wouldn't the paparazzi get a kick out of this? It makes our wedding very *different*, don't you think?"

"No, babe. It makes it very Josh and Riley."

She smiled at that, and the pieces of his heart scrambled back together.

"Now it makes sense that we had to run from the photographers and ditch your extended family to hide away in a big house where my mother and your sister and all the girls got so freaking high from Elisabeth's brownies that they were skinny-dipping and banging holes in walls and chanting and—"

Josh couldn't tell if she was angry, upset, or being sarcastic, but she was rambling about nonsense. He placed his hands on her shoulders, trying to slow the words flying from her mouth like bullets. "Riley, slow down. You're not making any sense."

She rolled her eyes. "Oh, yes, I am. Those brownies Elisabeth gave me were meant for a client, and laced with marijuana. Luckily I didn't eat any." She covered her belly with her hand. "But everyone else ate them, including my mother. They ate everything else in the kitchen, too. Then they proceeded to lose their freaking minds. I had to wake up the guys to take control of them. Oh, and Dane said you made arrangements for Beau to do some work for Charlotte?"

"Yes. I called him when we were looking over the terrace. We noticed there were some…" Josh was still trying to process what she'd said. "Wait. Holes in the wall? Really? Are they okay?"

"Yes, but *wow*. It was wild. I thought they were drunk, but Elisabeth texted and said she'd made medicinal brownies for a client and accidentally gave them to me."

Josh laughed, then quickly tried to school his expression. "I'm sorry. I don't mean to laugh, but—" Laughter bubbled up again, and before he knew it, Riley was laughing, too. "Your mother was high?"

"As a kite." Her smile reached her eyes, and when she glanced toward the dress, Josh's heart beat a little harder.

He took her hand in his and pressed a kiss to her knuckles, walking her over to the bed, where she sat on the edge. "Do you have any idea how much I love you, Riley Banks?"

"You must have a thing for girls with bad luck."

"I only have a thing for you, babe. Bad luck, good luck. I'll take it all. I hate what happened to your dress, but at the same time, it's apropos, don't you think?" He gently laid her down on her back and rolled her shirt up, exposing her belly.

She watched his fingers move softly over her belly, followed by his lips. She pushed her fingers through his hair.

"I missed you today," she whispered, breathing a little harder.

He moved over her, propping himself up on one forearm, and stroked her cheek as he kissed her. Several long, slow kisses later, he gazed into her eyes and said, "I've missed you, too. I'm sorry your pre-wedding night got messed up."

Pushing her shirt up further, he unhooked the front of her bra and pushed the lace cups to the side. "But I plan to make it up to you."

He slicked his tongue over one taut peak, and she inhaled sharply. Moving his mouth to her other breast, he ran his tongue in circles around her nipple, knowing how it drove her crazy. She writhed beneath him, rocking against his arousal.

"Josh," she pleaded, pulling his mouth down to her breast.

Sliding one hand down her hip, he clutched her ass as he pressed his erection against her center. She was trembling again, but this was a familiar tremble. An I-need-you all-over body shudder that he dreamed of and craved, and memorized. Her breathing shallowed as he teased her nipple with his teeth and tongue while thrusting his hips. She spread her legs wider, lifting her knees so her body cradled his. Damn, he wanted to strip her bare and take her fast and hard, but the frantic beat of her heart and the sexy, needy whimpers escaping her luscious lips were worth the slow burn.

"This is my last night with you as my fiancée, and I intend to enjoy every moment of it." He slanted his mouth over hers, taking her in a deep, passionate kiss and earning more greedy moans. As their mouths parted, he trapped her lower lip between his teeth and gave it a gentle tug. Their sex life had no boundaries, just the way he liked it. There was nothing they hadn't done, and tonight he wanted all of her.

He lifted her shirt over her head and made quick work of removing her bra and his shirt. She reached for the button on her jeans, and he took her wrist and placed it beside her hip.

"Let me." He kissed her again, a little rougher than before, just the way he knew she liked it. Her nipples pressed against his chest, and her hands moved up and down the back of his arms.

"Love when you touch me, baby."

He kissed his way down her body, spending extra time on each breast, teasing her until she was panting with desperation. He dragged his tongue down the center of her belly and used his teeth to pull open the button on her jeans. He unzipped them slowly, loving the quickening of her breath with each tick of the zipper. Riley curled her fingers in the sheets, straining as he hooked his fingers in the sides of her waistband and tugged her jeans and panties off.

"I will never tire of looking at you, baby." He stood at the end of the bed, drinking in the sight of her gorgeous curves and the sweet, slightly shy expression on her beautiful face as he removed his shoes and stripped her bare.

She sat up and wrapped her delicate fingers around his cock. When she lowered her mouth, taking him in deep, greedy pleasure burned through Josh's veins. She knew just how to touch him, with a tight grip following her lips as she took him to the back of her throat and then withdrew slowly. She repeated the motions, taking him right up to the edge of release. He squeezed the base of his cock, and she drew back.

"I want to come inside you, baby." He laid her down on her back, then ran his hands up the outside of her legs while kissing her inner thighs. "After I devour you."

She trapped her lower lip between her teeth the way she did when she was trying not to beg him to take her. He liked it when she begged; he also liked it when she *took* and *gave*. Sealing his teeth over her inner thigh, he gave her sensitive skin a hard suck.

"Josh," she pleaded, her hips bolting off the bed.

He held her hips, licking and sucking and kissing his way up to the juncture of her thighs, inhaling the seductive scent of her desire, and pushed her legs open wider. Her eyes were closed, her heart pounding so wildly her breasts moved with each beat.

"I love you, Riley June," he said before taking his first taste of her sweetness, and then there was no holding back. He loved her with his mouth and hands, moving with her as she bucked and writhed, begging and digging her nails into his shoulders as he took her up, up, *up*, until she finally lost her last shred of control. She came hard and loud. Thank Christ they were a wing away from the others. He craved the way she gave herself over to him, surrendering to their passion without embarrassment. He moved up her body, kissing every inch of her hot flesh, lingering around her belly, taking pleasure in knowing that deep inside her their baby was growing. When they were eye to eye again, the head of his cock resting against her slick heat, he gazed into her eyes and his heart swelled to near bursting.

"You are my *life*, baby. My love, my hopes, my dreams. My *everything*."

"Josh," she whispered. "You've always been my everything."

As their mouths came together and their bodies became one, the chaos of the day faded away.

Chapter Six

FROM THEIR PERCH on a lounge chair on the patio of the suite in the east wing where Riley and Josh had made love into the wee hours of the morning, Josh watched the sun creep over the mountains and pulled the covers around Riley. She snuggled closer, twining her legs with his. After too few hours of sleep, they'd taken a warm bath together—their last as an unmarried couple—and had gathered pillows and blankets and gone outside to watch the sunrise. The air was crisp, bringing the scents of pine, dew, and love.

Last night, when Riley had found out about her dress, she had been so edgy from the brownie madness, she hadn't felt the full impact of her ruined wedding gown. But on their way out to the patio she'd taken a good long look at her dress, mourning the loss of the perfect gown she and Josh had designed together. Josh had held her while she cried, whispering memories they'd created while they were designing the dress, and she'd realized, it wasn't the clean white skirt of the gown that had made the gown so perfect. It was the time they'd shared when designing it, the way they'd combined both of their ideas and poured their love into every aspect of the design process. It was heartbreaking for sure, but how upset could she really get over two sweet little boys trying to help her make her dress even *more* beautiful. Max and Bree might have little designers on their hands.

"We're getting married," Riley said softly, dragging her fingers along Josh's abs beneath the blanket.

"You're going to get lucky again if you keep doing that." He leaned down and kissed her.

She laughed, warmed by his adoration of her. His affections were endless, his gaze seductive, and his touch, well, her body was already stirring in all the best places just thinking about being naked beneath him again. But she had things to do this morning. With the craziness of the night before, she'd left the cake on the counter and she wanted to put it away before the kids or Josh saw it.

She pushed up, putting a little space between them before she changed her mind. "I have to go put the cake away."

He slid his warm hand up her arm. "I'll help you."

"Nice try." She leaned forward and gave him a chaste kiss. "This is my surprise to you. You've already indulged in one thing that was supposed to be saved for our wedding night. You're not getting the cake."

He tugged her back down on top of him. "I'd rather have seconds…I guess I mean sevenths…of you than a cake any day."

"Glutton," she said, thinking of all the ways they'd made love. Not an inch of her body had gone untouched.

"Only for you, babe."

His entrancing dark eyes summoned her closer, and he guided her hips over his. He rocked beneath her, pressing temptingly against her as he took her in a torturously slow, insanely electrifying kiss. Then his hands were on her ass, holding her tight against him as he thrust harder, and thoughts about the cake spiraled away. He pushed his hands down the back of her jeans, clutching her bare ass, and groaned into the kiss. God, she loved the way he made her world spin and her heart flutter. A flock of birds flew past, stirring the air and chipping away at her lust-addled brain.

"Josh," she said, breathless, as she pushed from his grip. "We can't."

"Oh, baby, we *can*." He pulled her close again, and she giggled as she struggled to be set free.

"The kids will see the cake," she said as he nibbled on her neck. "And then they'll want it, and their parents will be stuck trying to make them forget about it. We can't do that to them."

He looked up at her with a sinful, and somehow pouty, gaze that did hot and twisty things to her insides. The rising sun reflected in his eyes, and her mind drifted back to the reason she'd said no in the first place.

"I'm sure I'll hate myself for this." She peeled his hands off of her and pushed to her feet. "But we already have a decorated dress, and the girls will all have puffy eyes in our pictures from lack of sleep, I'm sure. At least let me hide the cake before we have crying kids to deal with, too. I'll come right back. I promise."

He held her hand as she moved away, and with a long sigh, he rose to his feet instead of letting go and tugged her against his chest again. His mouth claimed hers, making all of her best parts beg to stay. When their lips parted, she was dizzy with desire.

"I'll be waiting." He undid the button on his jeans and began unzipping them.

"Oh Lord. I'll be fast." With her heart sprinting in her chest, she turned and bolted from the room. Taking the stairs two at a time, she mentally planned how she would relocate the cake from the kitchen to the dining room and close the heavy wooden doors. When she reached the landing, she slowed her pace so as not to thunder through the main section of the house and wake anyone up. Walking quickly through the living room, her mind drifted back to Josh, and goose bumps rose on her flesh. She could still feel his lips on hers, his hands on her skin, his erection against her—

A high-pitched shriek snapped Riley out of her daze. She ran through the archway to the kitchen and stopped short at the sight of Max standing on a chair—and a handful of hissing raccoons scrambling off the counters and out of cabinets, sending the plates from last night's munchyfest—and what was left of Riley's wedding cake—careening to the floor with a loud *crash* as the four-footed savages scurried out the door to the terrace.

Max continued shrieking, and Treat barreled into the kitchen, followed by Rex, Jack, and Dane. Treat swept Max into his arms and carried her out of the room, passing Hugh and Hal on their way in.

"My cake!" Riley yelled, teetering on tiptoes. As if *that* would do any good against ravenous raccoons.

"Out of the kitchen," Jack commanded, and she was quick to obey, despite her ruined cake. She watched from just beyond the entryway as Max tried to catch her breath within the safety of Treat's arms just a few feet away. Jack and the others threw open cabinets and checked under furniture for any lingering rascals.

"We have to check the house," Rex said, and pointed to the living room, dining room, and the stairway that led to the bedrooms. Hugh, Hal, and Dane each took off in a different direction.

Please, please don't let there be raccoons near the children.

Jack reached for the door, and cursed loudly.

"What?" Riley backed up farther, fear rippling through every inch of her body. She envisioned droves of raccoons running toward Jack.

He turned dark, apologetic eyes toward her. "They climbed the canopy."

Her heart sank. The canopy? The drapes Josh sent back four times, until they were dyed the exact color he envisioned? Her eyes shifted to the bits of cake and broken dishes strewn across the counters and floor, and she reached for the wall to steady herself.

"Oh, Riley," Max said from behind her.

Riley couldn't stop the rush of tears springing from the corners of her eyes. A thick arm circled her shoulder, and Treat pulled her against his broad chest as she sobbed. She was vaguely aware of voices and footsteps as the others came downstairs. It was like all the forces of the universe were against their wedding taking place, and the raccoons were the straw that broke the camel's back. Suddenly all the sadness, all the confusion of the last twenty-four hours, which had been simmering somewhere deep inside her, hit the boiling point.

Nothing was going to stop her from marrying Josh.

Not a hole in a wall. Not decorations drawn by sticky little hands or a ruined cake. Not even a horde of raccoons would keep her wedding from taking place. *Goddamn raccoons. Ruined my cake. Ruined our canopy. What the hell else can go wrong?* She pushed from the safety of Treat's chest and wiped her eyes.

"Treat," she said harsher than she meant to. "Get ready to officiate our wedding."

"Riley," Jade said softly. "What…?"

Pushing past her mother, Jade, and Lacy, Riley stalked toward the stairs. "I don't care what else happens. It can rain so hard that we need Noah's Ark to survive, or a swarm of bees can attack us as we say our vows. I. Don't. Care. Our baby is going to have married parents!" She stormed down the stairs, too upset to care about the footsteps coming after her.

"Baby? Riley Roo—"

Oh shit. Did I say 'baby'? Shit, shit, shit.

Her mother's voice lingered in her ears as she descended the steps and walked quickly down the hall toward the suite where she and Josh had spent the night. She didn't care about the drapes or the cake or even the paparazzi, for that matter. Let them come and get all of this on video. None of that mattered.

"Baby?" Jade and Max said in unison, catching up to her, with Lacy and Savannah on their heels.

"You're pregnant?" Jade shifted little Hal on her hip.

Her mother was beside her now, too. Her concerned gaze boring into Riley.

Riley clenched her teeth together, shifting her eyes to the floor as she walked.

"Riley!" Jade grabbed her arm, slowing her down. "You're *pregnant* and you didn't tell me?"

The hurt in her best friend's eyes nearly brought her to her knees. "I…" The others were watching her intently, hanging on to her every word. She glanced at little Hal, whose wide dark eyes were moving between Riley and Jade.

A swarm of love and guilt tightened like a noose around Riley's neck. It was all she could do to choke out, "They said I couldn't get pregnant, and then I did. And you guys were so happy with your babies and adorable families, and Josh and I…We're hanging on to a shred of hope that our pregnancy will stick." Her throat nearly closed with her confession. She couldn't take it. It was all too much. She walked away on shaky legs.

"Riley," her mother called after her. "You thought you couldn't have children?"

The devastation in her mother's voice brought painful memories of the day she and Josh had received that awful news. Riley had cried for what felt like a week straight, and Josh had shed a river of tears, too. But she hadn't realized then that her mother must have experienced the same agonizing torture. She'd wanted a big family, but she'd never been able to conceive after having Riley. Riley slowed her stride, feeling a pang of guilt and sadness.

"Ri, that's *why* you need to share this with us," Jade implored. "You're my best friend, and it kills me to know you went through that alone. And now. Oh, Riley," she said sadly. "You must be scared to death. You don't have to go through this alone, too."

This slowed Riley down even further, because hadn't she known that all along? "But I'm not alone," she said softly. "I have Josh."

"It's not the same," her mother said gently. "Honey, nothing is the same as having the support of women who understand and have been where you are. As a woman who wanted a big family and ended up with just one perfect daughter"—she reached for Riley's hand and gave it a squeeze—"I understand what you're going through. Josh is the most important part of your life now, as he should be. But he can't know what it feels like to have life growing inside of you, so he can't know what it's like to be told you'll never give birth to a child. Not on the same level as a woman who knows what it's like to be willing to give your heart and soul in order for that life to thrive. We're here, baby girl. We're always here for you. Not to replace Josh. Just to accompany him in supporting you."

The noose pulled tighter, and worse, the truth of her mother's words brought another type of guilt. The realization that Riley had cut her best friend—*friends*—and her family out of this part of her life, not to spare their feelings but maybe to spare her own.

"I was scared," she said just above a whisper. "Talking about it makes it more real, and…" She glanced at Jade and little Hal, at Max, who was looking at her with so much empathy it made Riley's chest ache. Lacy and Savannah huddled closer with the same emotions written on their faces. "I was jealous, too, and that's ugly and hateful and so *wrong*." As they moved in to embrace her, her emotions threatened to suffocate her.

"I'm sorry," she said, turning away. "I can't…I just can't." She ran down the hall, ignoring their continued offers of support as they raced behind her, and threw the door to the suite open.

"Josh, I want to get married now, and—" Her legs stopped working at the sight of Josh lying on the bed with his arms crossed behind his head. Buck. Naked.

Max and Jade bumped into Riley's back, jolting her overloaded brain into panic mode.

"Oh shit." Josh jumped from the bed and scrambled into his briefs.

"Holy moly," Jade said.

"Perfect. Just flipping perfect." Riley threw her hands up in the air and turned around as Max and Jade ushered the others, who were peering around them to see what the fuss was about, out of the room, shouting, "Go, go, go!"

Jade turned as Riley tried to close the door and said, "Forget us. *Take* him!"

Riley closed the door, leaned her back against it, and covered her face with her hands. Too frustrated to laugh or cry, she made a garbled, mewing noise that rivaled the frantic sounds the raccoons had made earlier.

Josh planted one hand on either side of her head and pressed his body to hers. "Why did they see me naked?"

She whimpered from behind her hands.

"Baby, talk to me."

She spread her fingers apart and looked at his smiling face. All the anger drained from her body, and she dropped her hands. "Raccoons got the cake."

"Raccoons..."

"Mm-hm. And they ruined the drapes, and this would *never* happen in New York!"

"And everyone followed you down here because...?"

"I *might* have said something about being pregnant." She winced, but his smile widened. "I'm sorry. I don't know what happened. I lost my mind when everything got ruined...Wait. Why are you smiling?"

"Because I love you so much. When everything went to hell, your mind went straight to our unborn child." He brushed his lips over hers. "Baby, that's beautiful."

"Or neurotic," she offered. "Oh God, Josh. Max and Jade saw you *naked*."

"Yeah, that kind of sucks, but right now..." He reached behind her and locked the door. "I'm going to take all your stress away." He lifted her shirt over her head and tossed it to the floor. "We can worry about that later. Hugh says it's bad luck not to make love to your bride before the wedding."

"That's not exactly what he said." Shivers ran up her spine as he rid her of her bra and pulled her pants down to her ankles. "But the kitchen is a wreck, and your brothers and father and Jack are searching the house for raccoons."

"And they're quite capable of carrying out the search. Just this once, can't we be a little selfish?" He knelt and pulled off her remaining clothes, stripped from his briefs, and lifted her into his arms. Her legs wound around his waist as he lowered her onto his hard shaft. They both groaned at the deep, penetrating connection. Her entire body flamed, greedy for his love.

"Josh, we should help them," she said halfheartedly, trying to fight the lust coursing through her and do the right thing. Her back met the wall, and he thrust into her. "Oh *God* you feel good." Her good intentions were no match for their love. "We should…" *Be selfish. Be very, very selfish.*

"Later," he promised, thrusting harder. "I thought about making love to you the whole time you were gone, and nothing." He dragged his tongue along her lower lip. "*Nothing…*" He gyrated, grinding his cock exquisitely over all her sensitive nerves. "Is going to keep me from loving every ounce of stress out of your beautiful body."

"Yes," she pleaded, and he did. Loving her harder, deeper, and oh so perfectly. Obliterating her stress until all that was left was his sweet voice whispering sweet *everythings* in her ear and his hot body moving over her, inside her, around her, cocooning her from the rest of the world and righting all the upended pieces of herself.

Chapter Seven

AS THE DIMMING sun set over the picturesque mountains, Josh stood beside his siblings and father, who was his best man, in front of the altar they'd built. Cleaning up had taken all day, as did Riley's baking. Riley and her mother had worked together to make another wedding cake, and despite what happened to the first one, she still refused to let Josh take a peek before the wedding. The drapes had been clawed to shreds where the raccoons had climbed them and were ruined beyond repair, but that didn't stop Josh from creating the perfect arbor for their wedding. Layla, Adriana, and their mothers, helped gather enough wildflowers to cover the frame of the wooden structure. Rex found lattice in the woodshed and hung it between the legs of the frame, and with the help of their brothers and Jack, they meticulously strung more lights, which Charlotte had found in a storage room marked "Holiday Decorations," around the pretty wooden arbor. The chandelier still hung from the center, though part of one arm had broken off. Presumably from curious four-legged creatures.

The only four-legged creature Josh wanted to be around was Hope, who had appeared in his dreams last night. She'd been standing in the grass at the base of the stairs, as she was now, with a flower wreath the girls had made hanging around her thick neck. *Smiling.* It was a strange sensation to see a horse smile—and to think, even for a moment, that maybe he was the last to understand what his siblings must have known all along. It didn't matter if his mother was spiritually connected to the horse or a necklace, or even this place. All that mattered was that she was alive in their hearts, and of course because of that they'd see or sense her everywhere. He'd simply been too caught up in work and building a life to look beyond the forest to see the trees.

"Son."

A heavy hand on his shoulder pulled him from his thoughts, and he lifted his gaze to meet his father's serious dark eyes.

"I'm truly sorry about Riley's gown."

"I know, Dad. It's fine, really. They're kids, and you had your hands full. Riley will be the most gorgeous bride no matter what she wears."

"Second most gorgeous." His father winked. "You're the last of my kin to marry, and it marks the end of a part of my life I never wished away." He squeezed Josh's shoulder as his eyes moved over his brothers, then their wives, and Savannah, who was holding Adam in her arms. "I never wished it away, but with all these darlin' grandchildren, and now Riley formally coming into our family, and your son or daughter on the way, we all have a lot to look forward to."

Josh's throat thickened. Too choked up to speak, he nodded in agreement. His father and the rest of his family had been supportive and elated at their pregnancy news. This chaotic weekend had made him realize how much he wanted to live among family, regardless of the insanity that sometimes ensued. Nothing could replace family.

Treat, standing on Josh's other side, cleared his throat as Adriana and Layla stepped outside the house and onto the terrace wearing their pretty peach dresses and flower tiaras. They each held the hand of their younger brother, both of whom looked adorable in their khaki pants and white dress shirts. Christian and Dylan each carried a red velvet pillow with a wedding ring tied to a pretty white bow sewn into the center.

The four children made their way toward the altar, smiling like it was the happiest day of their lives—it was Josh's, that was for sure. Josh nervously patted the bulge in his pocket, where he'd hidden the key to the house on Rosedale Lane in Weston. He'd purchased it the week after they'd found out Riley was pregnant. It was supposed to be his wedding gift to Riley, so she'd have options and wouldn't feel the pressure to make a hasty decision one way or the other. Her parents had graciously offered to meet the furniture delivery trucks yesterday, a chore he couldn't have given to his brothers. Their wives were too curious, and the secret would have surely slipped out. They were strong, but Josh knew firsthand how strength melted beneath the warmth of true love. Now the key he'd been hiding would go undelivered. Riley had spent the day talking about how none of this would have happened if they'd married in New York— paparazzi or not. She didn't need to spell out her decision, and as much as Josh had been looking forward to raising his children close to family, at least part-time, Riley's happiness came first.

"Look, Uncle Josh! We didn't drop the pillows!" Dylan said proudly as he came to his father's side.

Treat put a hand on Dylan's shoulder.

"You carried them like champs," Josh said. He wondered if his little girl or boy would ever have a chance to walk down an aisle in support of their loved ones. Watching Layla smooth a wayward spike of hair on Christian's head tugged at his heartstrings, and he knew his and Riley's babies would always be surrounded by loving cousins, no matter how many miles separated them from day to day.

Riley stepped onto the deck beside her father in her newly decorated wedding gown. Her dark hair tumbled over her shoulders in gentle waves, and she proudly wore the headdress the girls had made. Josh lost his breath. And when Riley smiled, her eyes glistening with tears of joy, just as his were, he couldn't resist stepping forward and meeting her halfway.

"In a hurry?" she asked with a soft laugh that made him grin like a fool.

Damn he loved her laugh. "You have no idea." He was in a hurry, all right. The sooner she became his wife, the quicker his lips could meet hers.

RILEY WAS SHAKING like a leaf and trying her best to hide it, which was silly because she was surrounded by all the people she loved most. But when Josh crossed the deck, his eyes blazing a path to hers, her heart rate quickened and it refused to calm. He looked even more strikingly handsome than usual, and it had nothing to do with his dark suit and silver tie, or the pretty yellow rose boutonniere. No, it was the aura of love he radiated that made her heart beat like she'd taken a hit of speed.

"You look beautiful." Josh reached for her hands.

"So do you," she managed.

She didn't know how long they stood there holding hands and gazing into each other's eyes, but it was long enough for the women to begin whispering and the children to begin giggling.

Her father cleared his throat, snapping them out of their private bubble.

Josh blinked several times, as if he'd also been too caught up in her to think. "I'm sorry," he said to her father, but he made no move to walk away. His eyes found hers again, and he opened his mouth as if to speak. She swore time stood still, but he closed his mouth again and blew her a kiss before returning to Treat's side.

"I think your husband-to-be is quite ready, sunshine," her father said sweetly, and offered her his arm.

"Yes, Daddy." She looped her arm through his. "We've been ready forever."

On shaky legs, she walked across the deck, taking in the beautiful lights illuminating the dusky night and the happy faces of the men and women who she knew would go to the ends of the earth for them. *And for our baby.* She stopped beside her mother, a silent message of love and Riley's apology for withholding the news about her pregnancy passing between them. Earlier, after she and Josh had calmed her whirling emotions, they'd had a long talk with their friends and families, explaining why they'd kept the news of their pregnancy to themselves. Riley had come away feeling relieved and very, very loved.

When they reached Josh, her father kissed her cheek and whispered, "I wish you a lifetime of happiness, sunshine."

Tears welled in her eyes, and she blinked them away. *No tears during the ceremony*, she reminded herself. She'd already shed enough tears this weekend.

Her father, who had never seemed particularly macho to Riley, nodded at Josh. There was something in the way he did it, with a serious, almost magnetic expression, that commanded respect. His message was clear. *Treat my baby right, or you'll have me to deal with.* In that moment she realized that what her mother had said rang truer than ever. Her father might not be rugged, but he was strong in all the ways that mattered.

She glanced at her future husband, who was looking at her like she was his entire world, and she knew her father needn't worry. Just as Josh had promised on the day they'd become engaged, they were partners in love and in life. Forever.

AFTER THE CEREMONY and all the congratulatory hugs and well wishes, Treat and Rex carried the cake out to the table on the deck. Josh could not believe his eyes. The four-layer cake was as beautiful as if it had been professionally baked. He squeezed Riley's hand.

"You're not going to leave me to become a baker, are you?"

She shook her head, her eyes dancing with delight. "No, but I think I've made a decision about where I want to live, and I hope it doesn't cause you to want to leave me."

"Baby, nothing could ever cause that. I know you want to stay in New York."

"That's the sweetest thing I've heard all day," Savannah said.

Josh hadn't realized anyone could hear them. He glanced at Savannah and then returned his attention to his beautiful new wife, who had a confused look in her eyes.

"No, Josh. I want to move home."

"You do? Even after all you said about nothing like this happening in New York?"

"Yes!" she said loudly. "That's one of the reasons why I want to move back to Weston. I miss it, Josh. I miss my parents and your family and the wild, silly things that happen when we're all together."

Josh didn't think, didn't hesitate, as he swept Riley off her feet and twirled her around. The train of her dress flew out behind her…directly into the cake.

"No!" Treat lunged to catch it at the same time Jade hollered, "The cake!" and dove for it. They each caught one side of the tray the cake had been carried out on, just as the three top layers tumbled off, causing everyone to yell, "No!"—except Riley and Josh, whose mouths were too busy kissing and hearts were too swept up in love to care.

When their lips parted, Riley gazed at him with so much love in her eyes, even with the chaos exploding around them, he knew she was taking the toppled cake in stride. While the others were busy keeping the little boys from eating the cake that had spilled onto the terrace, worrying over the cake on Riley's dress, and joking about what else could go wrong, Josh reached into his pocket and withdrew the key.

"What's this?" Riley asked as he set it in her palm.

"It's the key to our new home in Weston. Your parents were late yesterday because the furniture delivery trucks got held up."

"You…Our new…?" Her damp eyes moved between Josh and her parents. "That's where you were?"

Her mother nodded.

Her father winked and said, "For you, sunshine. Just make sure you put locks on the bedroom doors. You never know when a surprise visitor will show up."

Riley gasped and shot a look at Savannah, whose cheeks were apple red.

"You weren't asleep?" Riley whispered to her father.

He shrugged. "I thought pretending to be was the polite

thing to do."

Everyone laughed, and her father gave Savannah a quick hug, assuring her that he hadn't seen a thing. Riley caught sight of Charlotte chatting with Lacy and Dane. She'd been so gracious about the damage they'd caused, and she'd even tried to talk Josh out of having his cousin Beau come fix the damage—along with a host of other things the men had deemed in need of repair. But she knew her husband, and there was no way he'd let her win.

My *husband.* She sighed dreamily. "Come here, *husband* of mine." Riley wrapped her arms around Josh's neck. "You're the most amazing man on the planet. Thank you. How did you know I'd want to live in Weston?"

"I didn't. I just wanted you to have options so you wouldn't spend the entire pregnancy worrying about it. The property's on Rosedale Lane, midway between our parents' homes, and it has a carriage house for our business, so the launch of your clothing line can be handled without missing a beat."

"Rosedale?" Hugh arched a brow. "*You're* the asshat?"

Josh grinned at his younger brother. "Sorry, bro."

"No, you're not," Hugh said.

"If I'd told you, your wife would have found out, and it wouldn't have been long after that before the grapevine found its way to Riley. Look at this radiant smile," he said, stroking Riley's cheek and earning an even bigger one. "You're right, Hugh. I'm not sorry about a damn thing."

Hal

HAL BRADEN HAD listened intently as his last son to marry said his vows, promising endless love to the woman he adored—and unearthing mountains of unexpected emotions in Hal. Now, as he watched his boys razzing each other, just as they'd done for too many years to count, a gentle breeze whispered over his skin. He lifted his eyes, catching sight of Hope looking up at him. His mind reeled back four decades to the day he'd taken Adriana as his wife. To the nervous, elated seconds before she'd said her vows. Her eyes had glistened with love. Her dark auburn hair had danced like a wild mane around her beautiful face as she'd stepped closer, so close the breeze carried her unique and alluring scent. A scent he smelled to this very day, in every whisper of the wind. His chest swelled now just as it had then, with love so impossibly all-consuming, he didn't know how he'd survive it. He remembered the way she'd gone up on her tiptoes right there in front of their family and closest friends, and she'd whispered in his ear.

And now, among the company of their family and closest friends, it was Adriana's sweet voice he heard whispering in his ear, the very same words she'd whispered so long ago. "Our family will never know any boundaries, Hal Braden. It's too big, too magnificent. It's *boundless*, just like our love."

Want More Bradens?

If this is your first Braden book, you might want to read Josh and Riley's love story, FRIENDSHIP ON FIRE (The Bradens at Weston), a full-length novel, or start with the very first Love in Bloom book, SISTERS IN LOVE (FREE at the time of this printing). All of my novels may be enjoyed as stand-alone romances. Jump in any time!

New to the Love in Bloom series?

The Love in Bloom big-family romance collection features several families. Characters from each series appear in future Love in Bloom books. All Love in Bloom books may be enjoyed as stand-alone novels or as part of the series.

Download FREE first in series books here:
www.MelissaFoster.com/LIBFree

Find free downloadable series reading order, publication order, family trees, and more on Melissa's Reader Goodies page:
www.MelissaFoster.com/RG

More Books By Melissa

LOVE IN BLOOM SERIES

SNOW SISTERS
Sisters in Love
Sisters in Bloom
Sisters in White

THE BRADENS at Weston
Lovers at Heart
Destined for Love
Friendship on Fire
Sea of Love
Bursting with Love
Hearts at Play

THE BRADENS at Trusty
Taken by Love
Fated for Love
Romancing My Love
Flirting with Love
Dreaming of Love
Crashing into Love

THE BRADENS at Peaceful Harbor
Healed by Love
Surrender My Love
River of Love
Crushing on Love
Whisper of Love
Thrill of Love

THE BRADEN NOVELLAS

Promise My Love
Our New Love
Daring Her Love
Story of Love

THE REMINGTONS

Game of Love
Stroke of Love
Flames of Love
Slope of Love
Read, Write, Love
Touched by Love

SEASIDE SUMMERS

Seaside Dreams
Seaside Hearts
Seaside Sunsets
Seaside Secrets
Seaside Nights
Seaside Embrace
Seaside Lovers
Seaside Whispers

BAYSIDE SUMMERS

Bayside Desires

The RYDERS

Seized by Love
Claimed by Love
Chased by Love
Rescued by Love
Thrill of Love

SEXY STANDALONE ROMANCE

Tru Blue
Truly, Madly, Whiskey

BILLIONAIRES AFTER DARK SERIES

WILD BOYS AFTER DARK
Logan
Heath
Jackson
Cooper

BAD BOYS AFTER DARK
Mick
Dylan
Carson
Brett

HARBORSIDE NIGHTS SERIES
Includes characters from the Love in Bloom series
Catching Cassidy
Discovering Delilah
Tempting Tristan
Chasing Charley
Breaking Brandon
Embracing Evan
Reaching Rusty
Loving Livi

More Books by Melissa
Chasing Amanda (mystery/suspense)
Come Back to Me (mystery/suspense)
Have No Shame (historical fiction/romance)
Love, Lies & Mystery (3-book bundle)
Megan's Way (literary fiction)
Traces of Kara (psychological thriller)
Where Petals Fall (suspense)

Meet Melissa

www.MelissaFoster.com
www.MelissaFoster.com/Newsletter
www.MelissaFoster.com/Reader-Goodies

Melissa Foster is a *New York Times* and *USA Today* bestselling and award-winning author. Her books have been recommended by *USA Today's* book blog, *Hagerstown* magazine, *The Patriot*, and several other print venues. Melissa has painted and donated several murals to the Hospital for Sick Children in Washington, DC.

Visit Melissa on her website or chat with her on social media. Melissa enjoys discussing her books with book clubs and reader groups and welcomes an invitation to your event.

Melissa's books are available in paperback and digital formats.

CPSIA information can be obtained
at www.ICGtesting.com
Printed in the USA
LVOW10s1816230617

539175LV00001B/107/P